MK-ULTRA

MK-ULTRA

*A tale of one family, the
CIA and the War on Drugs*

Judith Nagib

To order additional copies of this book, contact:
Xlibris Corporation
1-888-7-XLIBRIS
www.Xlibris.com
Orders@Xlibris.com

CONTENTS

Dedicated to Brahim.

ACKNOWLEDGMENTS

I wish to acknowledge Tom Greening's authorship of Tarif's poem as well as his inspiration for many ideas in this novel and his support of the author's efforts in creating it.

I would also like to mention my appreciation for all I have learned from law firms which continue the practice of offering pro bono assistance to indigent non-violent drug offenders. They are the real heroes of the War on Drugs.

Judith Nagib
September 2000, Chicago

Chapter One

Two Afternoons in the Middle East

The Moqqatam Highway winds its way up between dusty hills from the flat, broad, and congested avenues of Cairo proper, roiling with clusters of people of all ages and genders-their costumes often exotically striking but just as often familiarly Western. The steady cacophony engendered by the crowds was occasionally surpassed in intensity by a symphony of feverish honking from a car population which collectively comprised the most oppressive traffic conditions in the world. Turbaned men in gallabeyahs intermingled with their more Europeanized counterparts in a completely unselfconscious merging. Those women referred to as "harim" (a combined nuance of forbidden, protected, and revered), presented a similar contrast to their less conservative sisters, who were becoming disturbingly plentiful in Cairo the past few years. And why not? These differences were only cosmetic, after all. People were equal in the sight of God.

Motoring this route could be a pleasant yet strange experience, like being in the cast of an unclassifiable movie-was it an obscene or esthetic experience? More often it was wearisome and annoying, to be negotiated as quickly as possible. It all depended on the temperament and schedule of the drivers on any particular day, who themselves were influenced in a fundamental way by the mood in the street, which was in turn shaped by a peculiar aggregate of the weather, that morning's coffee, one's wife's mood the evening before, and above all, by international politics. For in Cairo, traffic had a personality. The cars behaved as if they had a life separate from the drivers. They could be audacious like a pampered Egyptian child or stoic and unbudgeable like a Middle Eastern grandmother.

On this particular summer evening, Hassan Nebilla's aging sedan, with so many chassis repairs it resembled an automotive patchwork quilt, ambled along at an uneven pace as he intermittently slowed to enjoy the ambience, a practice which he considered his indelible right as an Egyptian citizen, and one in which he indulged several times an hour. Now, approaching a fork in the road which led either to the summit of an imposing hill on the right, or to the airport on the left, Hassan Nebilla made a sharp right, glancing at Saladin's Wall, as he always did. The Wall was a crumbling medieval edifice-resplendent in its steadfast survival, outlasting the competition in the neighborhood: gravestones, mosques and ancient residences in varying stages of decay, collectively giving the impression of a gigantic, impenetrable slum which was, in some ineffable way, dignified. Concerning the Wall, legend has it that the great Saladin, pursued by bands of enemies from all sides, and with all available routes to escape blocked, exhorted his gallant Arabian steed to leap over the Wall in a sort of medieval kamikaze operation. Offering up one's life, human or otherwise, was and still remains, in the Middle Eastern soul, the sine qua non of obedience for subordinates toward their masters. Of course it meant certain death for the horse. Yet, with his unwavering loyalty, the unflinching stallion, in one breathtaking moment, cut his last astonishingly beautiful silhouette across the Egyptian sky as he leaped into the air. Saladin survived to become a living martyr to the masses. A great story recited with poignant emotion by aristocrats and beggars alike from time immemorial at rituals, very often at Ramadan, and at various other times of the year between coffee, and to every foreigner at any time at all. There were no variation of the story that Hassan Nebilla had ever heard. Too, variations of myths were banned as sacrilegious, after all. As predictable as the plot of Saladin's tale, was the visceral display of emotions elicited at its conclusion, usually in the form of an unavoidably noticeable stream of tears down faces on which the tightly-drawn tense lips and furrowed brows seemed permanent. These faces, so unabashedly eager to be transformed by sentimentality, were peculiarly mostly male and only infrequently female. Women in that society had grown remarkably resilient (yet still respectful or perhaps fearful of) the power of legends to control men's behaviors and destinies. The fierce loyalty and heroism of the Arabian horse touched a deep vein in them also, however primordial and archetypal it was. Raconteurs were no less susceptible to its thrills and power to evoke deep emotion despite the fact that it had been memorized very early in life and already recited hundreds of times. They remained staunchly uninured by relentless exposure to the legend. The residual raw passion was perceived, certainly not at all as a form of naivete, but rather as honor when felt in oneself and strength of character when observed in others.

Foreigners new to the area, especially entrepreneurial types on assignments for their Western companies, found it a curious thing. To the seasoned emigres, however, it was all part of the Zeitgeist. The nouveau found it difficult to comprehend the ingenious ability of the Egyptian to evoke intense feelings at a moment's notice. One theory, popular among anthropologists, sociologists and cross-cultural psychologists, was that the starkness of the desert surrounding Egypt had an enormous influence in the shaping of a personality so that the end product was nearly devoid of the ability to comprehend ambiguity or the occasional necessity to compromise one's principles. As a result, the only two acceptable publically expressionable emotions were harsh stoicism (which the cross-cultural psychologists classified as a "collective defense mechanism", an undifferentiated sentimentality (which the tourist of Western origin misunderstood and described to neighbors and friends, fellow Church-goers as well as anyone else who would listen, as "charming".) Publicly exhibited anger was also, but to a lesser extent, a sign of strong conviction, provided it was highly orchestrated, controlled, and rehearsed, for maximum effect.

None of this had been lost to the American businessman who

constantly grappled with the enticing opportunity of possibly harnessing this immense reservoir of bipolar energy so as to direct it toward the purchase of good, preferably American, instead of toward the fomenting of political discord. Social scientists, however, envisioned quite another use for it, to more constructive ends, such as the recognition of women's rights, laws requiring mandatory education for *every* child through secondary school (including the fellaheen children-in which case the corps of twelve-year-old maids in Cairo would be depleted), the building of labor rather than capital-intensive factories, and the acceptance of the concept of a minimum wage. Eventually, sooner or later, a hypnotic resignation overcame those zealous reformers, be they capitalists or promiscuous altruists. It was the inevitable fate of everyone who had the fortune or misfortune, depending on the outcome, of spending more than six months in this relic of a country, inching along at a snail's pace, if not quite into the future, then at least into that evening and with luck, into the next day.

A transaction which might normally take an hour anywhere else in the world except perhaps India, takes at least three in Cairo, for no immediately apparent reason. Yet the sense of a great daily buzz of activity permeated the city. This incongruity between the appearance of energetic effort and the dismal result of it was initially the biggest disappointment for most foreigners. Adaptation varied, depending on the country of origin, with the typically compulsive Americans and Germans being the last to finally relinquish, though agonizingly and bitterly, their self-discipline in the face of relentless apathy.

Daily schedules habitually fell apart by noon. They were constructed according to the discipline of the hours available to complete a certain task, not by unpredictable events and certainly not by the vagaries of a person's emotions. Time was transformed from a system of minutes and hours to what could be possible after breakfast but before siesta time, or between tea and dinner. Entropy flourished everywhere. It took half a day to send a telex. There seemed to be no particular reason. The machines worked.

The numbers were correct. Somewhere a glitch in the system existed, but where? A sense of the gargantuan, monstrously complicated relational reality which existed behind the scenes in Egypt's social circuitry, keeping the system working, barely, but also keeping it from changing, was eventually dimly perceived, but never completely, by the foreigner with his penchant "to understand"-as if everything could be solved by "understanding" it. Such naivete! thought the indigenous intelligentsia, who were an odd collection of scholars and illiterate philosophers. Newly transferred executives and their wives continued to protest living conditions even after the hope that innovative complaining might bring results had long elapsed. Nonetheless, they went on visiting their embassies, writing letters to the *Herald Tribune*, and demanding amenities which they had formerly taken for granted, such as shower curtains, functioning air conditioning, the minimum amount of electric power to be able to read an article with normal sized fonts, and flushable toilets.

The home companies deferred to local landlords who resembled emasculated congressmen, given to much polemic, compassion and commiseration, but who were unable to accomplish anything. Some temporary Western residents never relinquished certain habits which appeared humorously odd and superfluous to everyone else. Jogging was one of those, a bastion of unfettered individual liberty identified with Western individuality. Indulging in such highly eccentric activities served as good a reminder as any that the semblance of freedom still existed despite the Egyptian bureaucracy, or perhaps because of it, which snuffed out the most resilient foreign habits.

The historical method of erosion of lifestyles not amenable to the Cairene milieu was the "governmental decree." Because of the proliferation of such decrees in Cairo, the possibility that it might someday be necessary, in order to secure one's right to jog a predetermined distance-safely-to complete a form, and submit it to the scrutiny and whims of an official stationed at some corner in the neighborhood, continued to loom as a nightmarish governmental option. But it was all for naught. Those pockets of liberty were allowed to remain as mere illusions of personal freedom so long as they did not attract the attention of the collective awareness, overwhelmingly defined by what in America is called *the critical mass.*

Magnificent ruins and temples, often superimposed on one another, existed in abundance and functioned as reminders of past splendors but had, unfortunately, long ago lost their power to galvanize the populace into concerted, effective action to change anything. The quintessential Egyptian, including the dutiful Bowab Hassan Nabilla, simple wanted to get by in life; a vision beyond mere survival meant change, and that brought with it the anxiety of facing an uncertain future as opposed to one which was predictable and secure.

The risk involved in the acceptance of change as a goal, let alone the energy to accomplish it, was an unacceptable price to pay for a reward whose immediate effects were perceived as tenuous at best. The social structure was thus imprisoned in a hierarchy of mere basic needs. It was difficult enough for the average fellahin to meet his family's requirements for food, safety and shelter. Therefore, what would be viewed as primary, but nevertheless lower-order needs (in First World countries) became the *basic* needs for most Egyptians. This view of existence, common in countries similar to Egypt, produced a population which functioned adequately yet myopically, never really able to shift the considerable pride in some Golden Age to the present. A mere shift of focus from the miserable present to the glorious past was necessary but not sufficient. Oh, to live as the Pharaohs, who built pyramids and temples which remain the wonder of the world, invented the numeric script, and who preserved the ancient knowledge which was to become the source of the Renaissance. No society could possibly accomplish such progress across such a wide spectrum of time again and culture again. Why try now? Even the Americans, adored and feared for their daring innovativeness, were nowhere near the accomplishments of that historical era, despite the fact that they had ushered in the computer revolution, cable TV, cellular phones, and transformed the concept of the European shopping gallerias into Malls-environments where human beings from infancy to senility could live in harmony, like a Woody Allen experiment, surrounded by conspicuous consumption.

Hassan Nebilla began the series of hairpin turns on the right fork of the Moqquattam Highway which would take him and the other occupants of the 1960 Austin sedan, two incessantly giggling women in the back seat, to their destination at the summit, as the Boss had instructed. Americans were the real losers, he mused, though they presented a facade of happiness and contentment, purchasable by dollars. Of course they would never admit their decadence. But all one had to do was to witness the divorce rate in America, which had reached 70% at least in California. That most enigmatic of American states presented a dilemma for Hassan. Its fecundity was simultaneously admired yet despised, a puzzle as stupefying to him as to the average Cairene, who was paradoxically both the victim and perpetrator of his own feckless government. Hassan concluded that American women are considered unequal by their men—despite loud protestations to the contrary—(that is why they often divorce), while Egyptian women, who are guaranteed equality under Islamic law even before they enter the conjugal union, experience a parity in role interaction with their husbands quite unknown in American life.

However, Westerners could never view the complex Arab world in a positive way because of their cultural superiority complex. Attempts to learn from the past were doomed to failure, since the past is continuously reconstructed to the advantage of the West, through tools such as the *research study* and the *cinema*. There, truth is edited in order to present the Third World to the First World as filled with backward people who, by inertia and the enslavement of their fellow men throughout history (although they were not unique in that practice), were able to achieve a decent standard of life, but only for a brief period, and who now languish in poverty and inefficiency.

If only our great teachers and leaders from Al Azhar University could reach their hearts, Hassan thought, they would surely change. The great mullahs had the ability to turn the hardest stone to honey by their great logic and compassion. It was never too late. Perhaps the paths to their minds could then be grasped through proper exposure to the Islamic system of equality as it was envisioned by the Prophet. Yet, there was a vast ideological chasm between theory and practice, it was true. The abolishment of the women's movement in Egypt by the government several years ago resulted in the outrage of liberal-thinking people worldwide. The rearranging of facts by the international press at that time insured a continued discussion of the poor state of human rights in Egypt, much to the country's chagrin.

Americans forget everything sooner or later. Egyptian women had brought it all on themselves, after all. In the midst of the liberation hysteria, they had begun emulating Americans in their shrill denunciations of male supremacy, causing much unnecessary consternation among their shocked fathers, husbands, and brothers. Eventually, but only with great difficulty and much anguish, they were brought back to the righteous path. In retrospect they were able to realize that all so-called radical liberals, in their zeal to achieve power, were doomed to fail. There was no quarrel with ambition. Women could certainly attain high achievements through and by motherhood, as was illustrated by countless examples in the tradition.

Why, it was recorded where Arab mothers had led armies into battle. Accomplishments which were unattainable because of the time necessary for pregnancy and nursing babies could be enjoyed vicariously through one's children. Motherhood indeed was a woman's greatest achievement! There was none higher. Every knew that. And because of that irrefutable truth, attempts to alter the sacred family structure were doomed to fail in Egypt. Many of Hassan's colleagues aspired to the American dream of the "Self-Made Man", but in no way did the activities resulting from that dream, such as travel abroad or intermittent separations from their wives and children, affect the family in a negative way. Consider the many Egyptian men who work and study abroad. Rarely do their homes disintegrate as a result. Men can resist temptation.

Women, however, fundamentally emotional and impressionable creatures, must be protected from ideas which might cause them harm, should their contemplation lead them to question the value of their exalted status. To avoid delusional thoughts of this type, the focus of the female should always be directed toward the Golden Age of the past, the time of the Pharaohs, when Egyptian civilization was at its pinnacle. Only men, at that historic juncture, were capable of temporarily adapting a future-orientation without denying tradition. This was possible because of the unswerving commitment to the stability of their families, instilled in them by *their* mothers.

It is obvious that women should remain anchored in the present by remaining committed to the responsibilities of children and homemaking. Philosophical yearnings could, after all, be satisfied by endlessly, continuously, and redundantly studying the past. The system therefore perpetuates itself. Her reward, were it to be acknowledged as such, was the immense respect of all men, for her voluntary relinquishment of two basic human rights: the choice of an attitude and the construction of her life in a future as she chooses to define it.

Future orientation in fact was systematically eliminated from her agenda, deemed inappropriate by her male caretakers, not worthy of her contemplation. It would only confuse her. In Egypt the future had a gender, and it was male. Men had become its explorers if not yet its transformers. The past, however, was androgynous: male myths perpetuated by female caretakers. Both sexes supported the accepted version of history. The traditional feminine role, gallant and heroic in unending servitude, was very much like Saladin's horse, forever entombed in a silhouette across the sky, a metaphor for the nobility of blind self-destruction in the service of a worthy master. Enlightened self-interest in the service of self, however, of survival, was not a noble option for a woman, who, to be considered virtuous, must always sacrifice for others, must always deny herself. The horseman's reward? More adventures, more challenges, more loves. In a word, Life itself. The animal is obliterated. That is the lesson children absorb into their memories, their identities, their mental chromosomes, while growing up in the Cairo of Hassan Nebilla. They do more than simply *learn* it, they *ingest* it, some say into their very DNA, ready to be passed on to the next generation. The heroic tale might differ, but the lesson was always the same.

Having amused himself for forty-five minutes in his favorite preoccupation, silent philosophizing (his family nicknamed him the "Father of Philosophers") and since there did not appear to be any over deviances from tradition for him to challenge this particular evening, Hassan Nebilla did not mind the sound of harmless joy emanating from the back seat of the car: the constant laughter, the rapid, animated "American" conversation. The two women were Westerners, after all, who were not raised to appreciate the pleasing effect on men that a woman's silence could bestow.

About the older woman, Hassan could not discern anything, except that she had very unusual eyes. They were green with tinges of yellow, the most striking component of her appearance. Otherwise she appeared very ordinary. He found himself, however, drawn again and again to those eyes, sometimes forgetting the road and then chastising himself. She probably had no honor at all, otherwise, why would she be traveling without a man, he thought, to accompany her and protect her? The younger woman was less auspicious, having lived in Egypt for a year. Her inclination toward virtuous living was reflected in less aggressive mannerisms in her behavior, but more importantly, she was more conservative and less provocative in her demeanor. Hassan credited the wisdom and patience of the Boss in that regard.

At that moment, in fact, the laughter and aggressive conversation reached a higher level and continued at a feverish pitch, until it seemed that all pretensions of modesty and virtue were rapidly disappearing. The younger woman began to display, to an alarming degree, a vitality which Hassan Nebilla had not seen since her arrival in Cairo, straight from the "West". She would definitely need what the Boss half-jokingly called "continued personality adjustment"-probably to occur after the older woman left. The Boss promised Hassan that someday he would explain what that term meant, so that perhaps he too could employ it to control others under his care. How often today had he wished he already knew it, for ever since the American woman had arrived, tension had become almost unbearable in the household. The boss said she needs to learn his priorities quickly, so he elected not to return her calls from her hotel until just this morning, after her seventh day in Egypt. That way *he*, not *she* would be in control. That was always an important point of strategy for him, and it was what the Boss initially sought in every confrontation: control of others, their deference to him. His methods to attain this might vary from situation to situation, but never the goal, which he invariably achieved.

Hassan smiled in unabashed admiration for him. Establishing dominance over others could best be obtained by what the Boss called "the cessation tactic." If someone foolishly interrupted one of the Boss' monologues, he or she would be confronted with a hostile stare of pure hatred, a look so frightening, a face so grimacing, that the thought of it made Hassan shudder. It was enough to silence most contenders for attention. Oddly, though, it had not worked immediately on the younger woman when she first arrived, and he was not sure of its effect on the older one should it be necessary to evoke it this evening.

It simply proved that females were a tremendous responsibility, he concluded, with all that necessity to censor their thoughts and actions in order to preserve the honor of the household. A rumor could, after all, be more damaging than an actual fact. Therefore, harshness was occasionally necessary, condoned in fact, in order to establish, beyond any doubt, the impeccability of the family's reputation. If discipline were accepted by women in the righteous manner in which it was intended by the men who administered it, if they would realize that it was for their best interests, for their protection, there could be great rewards for them, vacations, cars, televisions! If not, however, everyone suffered, but the woman most of all, from the ill-feelings and bad will of the entire society toward her, and toward her family, upon whom her behavior reflected.

It was not a step to be taken lightly. What was the point in resisting? In the Boss' case, there were practically no limits to his generosity to the faithful circle of family and friends. Likewise, there were none to his ferocity against those who wavered from the path of righteousness as he defined it. Hassan prayed that the older woman would leave soon, so that these variations which she was creating in their otherwise calm household, by her presence, would vanish, and tranquility and predictability would once again prevail. Sudden changes in routine are to be viewed with extreme suspicion.

At last they arrived at the alfresco restaurant near the Mohammed Ali Mosque, a beautiful edifice atop the Moqqattam Hills, one of the Boss' favorite spots. There he was, in fact, standing grim-faced next to the boy, his constant companion. Hassan worried that his lateness was the cause of the Boss' look of consternation, and he was prepared to embellish his explanation that the frivolities of the two women while they were at the hotel had caused their delay. They exchanged knowing glances. Hassan believed in his heart that the Boss, in his tremendous natural wisdom, understood everything intuitively and instantly.

Suddenly, the older women, in a show of incredible boldness and unabashed spontaneity, opened the car door herself-without waiting for Hassan to do it-and ran past the Boss to the boy, embracing him shamelessly in front of everyone. Such audacity! The Boss looked on sternly and silently. The younger woman emerged from the car slowly, and then they all entered the Moqqattam restaurant together, following the Boss' lead. The boy unhesitatingly sat down next to the older woman and appeared unusually cheerful as he, like the younger woman, began talking and laughing incessantly. The older woman, whoever she was, had the strange effect on people of stimulating in them an unsettling sense of abandon. Hassan was beginning to be affected by it too. He was actually smiling in spite of himself.

The Boss, after a brief departure to the restaurant's kitchen, gave Hassan a sharp reprimand when he noticed his grin, then motioned to a servant to come forward carrying a huge tray of appetizers in the form of hummus and mahshi, stuffed tiny vegetables. He took one of the individual plates of hummus and set it in front of the older woman. The significance of this act was not lost on Hassan. The first person served was someone of great importance, by custom. Perhaps Hassan had underestimated her. Who was she? The Boss continued to distribute plates filled to the brim with food. He however, was apparently not staying for dinner. Instead, he stood at the head of the table for a few moments, surveying the scene in that calm, self-assured way he adapted while in complete control, with everyone conforming to his wishes. Hassan sighed in relief. Perhaps it would be a quiet uneventful evening after all.

Suddenly the Boss turned, strode over to him, directing him to stand guard at the only door to the restaurant. He said that Hassan must not allow the two women or the boy to leave. The Boss would return in two hours. He repeated, as if it were a threat, *they are not to leave*! Okay, Boss, okay, Hassan thought. Yet he never questioned him, whom he regarded as undecipherable, and whose reasons went far beyond the capacity of anyone to understand. So, why bother to ask? Better to accept, obey, and be rewarded.

During the ensuing two hours, Hassan Nebilla observed a marathon of talking and giggling, apparently pointless, from the two women and the boy. Given such familiarity, the older woman must somehow be related to the boy and the young woman. How else to explain such intimacy? "Blood is always thicker than water", said Hassan Nebilla to himself, a proverb always uppermost in his mind when assessing situations involving family, friends and strangers.

A loyal friend of many decades might be cast aside in favor of an insufferable relative. That was the choice that had to be made, if society were to remain cohesive. The Boss had told him that the children's mother had died years ago, so the older woman's relationship was clearly not maternal. Could she be a maternal aunt, perhaps? The boy had described his mother often to Hassan Nebilla, but he never mentioned the green eyes with yellow flicks in them, the woman's most striking feature. Surely that would have been mentioned in her physical description.

Hassan decided, given the deference and affection being lavished on her, that she must surely be related to the dead mother. He longed to ask exactly what that relationship was, but he had not been invited to join them for dinner at their table. As usual, Americans were insufferably rude. He had to bribe the fellahin waiters for his dinner, while he waited for what seemed an interminable time for the Boss to return and for this silly chatter and nonsense to stop. Despite the inappropriateness of their behavior, he found himself charmed to see the boy and the young woman so overtly happy in the older woman's presence. Who was she? Hassan promised himself to be especially ingratiating to the Boss the following week in the hope of solving this mystery.

As the evening slowly wore on, the boy and the two women were served course after course of barbecued chicken and lamb, stuffed vegetables of various kinds, eggplants, yogurt and desserts to tempt even the most discriminating of palates. The Boss had really outdone himself this evening, in terms of generosity. It was a superb Middle Eastern meal and Hassan hoped that the older women, whoever she was, appreciated it. The only possible discomfort they might suffer was that caused by the swarms of mosquitos descending on them at dusk and which were legendary in the Moqqattam Hills. The boy seemed particularly affected by them, often getting up from his chair and in general seeming fidgety. Perhaps he was also unnerved by the presence of the strange woman.

Finally, all the food was consumed, quite a feat in an Egyptian restaurant where the quantities served were gargantuan even by

American standards. Hassan was enjoying the after dinner ambience and coffee. Perhaps this woman was not so bad after all, he thought. She encouraged the children's appetites, always a good thing, and made them laugh. Was that bad?

Jolted from his reverie, Hassan turned quickly at the sound of the heavy footsteps of the Boss. Had two hours passed already? The boy and the young woman did not hide their extreme disappointment at his arrival, but obediently got up and left the dining area at his signal, slowly walking toward the car and furtively glancing back at the older woman who now sat alone, motionless, smiling silently. The Boss, ignoring her, questioned Hassan in minute detail about all that had transpired since his departure, listening intently, particularly to references of the older woman. When was each course served? Was anything else ordered to drink or eat? Did the woman behave normally? Did she use the restroom at any time? After listening to Hassan's staccato responses, the Boss suddenly stood once again at the head of the table, engaging the older woman in animated conversation. They were shouting at each other, both very agitated. The younger woman and the boy, who were hanging around the doorway instead of going on, looked frightened. There was no laughter now. The Boss suddenly turned, shouting at them to go to the car as they were ordered, and to wait there. Immediately they scurried off like trained pets.

Finally the entire party left, the Boss leading the way and Hassan walking swiftly behind the older woman, who wore on her face a look of extreme discomfort. Hassan was instructed to drive her back to her hotel. They would then both return several hours later to take her to Cairo Airport for her flight back to the United States. The Boss slammed the door of his late model BMW, turned on the ignition, lights, and radio, and squealed out of the parking lot in a cloud of dust. The young woman and the boy in the back seat did not look back.

Together in the old sedan, which seemed even drabber now, compared to the BMW, Hassan proceeded down the steep hill with the older woman, who, in another brazen act, had seated herself in the front of the car rather than in the back, as all respectable women would normally do. Her demeanor had changed dramatically. She wore a steely expression and seemed paler than before, in the Egyptian moonlight. Gone was the infectious smile he noticed in the restaurant. Finally arriving at the hotel, she slammed the car door behind her, not saying goodnight nor looking back. Hassan drove slowly back to the Boss' family complex, feeling oddly sad and as perplexed as ever.

Soon enough, however, he was returning at 4 A.M. with the Boss to the same hotel. It was time to take the older woman to the airport. She was already waiting out in front with her bags. The steely expression had not changed. Hassan much preferred her the other way, with that peculiar admixture of spontaneous emotion and positive self-assurance which he had noticed before and during dinner at the Moqqattam Restaurant. The Boss kept questioning her about the exact time of her flight, which route she planned to take to Los Angeles, and whether there would be any stops along the way. Then apparently satisfied, he lapsed into a cold silence, not looking at the woman again until she collected her things at the airport and without a word, left the car with the door still open and headed for the security check in site, ignoring the many offers of hustlers who functioned as self-appointed skycaps. Her expression remained harsh and determined, green eyes flickering. The Boss was equally stern and resolute. At that moment, it occurred to Hassan that she was the Boss' match in some strange way that he could not understand, and he found himself admiring her. But the question of her identity continued to dog him.

Jerusalem

Like an esprit de l'escalier, the whimsical cool north wind rushed around corners creating skirmishes with pedestrians who were least expecting them, ruffling their hair, forcing them to squint, clutch their collars, suck in their breaths, and murmur, "that wind!" The brilliant sunshine with its scintillating effect on windowpanes, tree branches and rooftops had a mitigating effect on the harsh mistral. The overall ambience was much like that on a fall afternoon somewhere on the Eastern Coast of the United States, most likely an urban area, given the shoppers bustling about that particular day in Jerusalem, like so many busy scuttling ants. The scene replicated that astounding American pastime, unrestrained shopping, so unlike the European method of close scrutiny, turning the purchase of an item of furniture into an occasion for conversation at dinner. No, the Americans were hostage to their habits of instant gratification and simultaneous sensory overload. The difference here, however, was that these Middle-Eastern modern malls were subtly constructed to discourage, without outright disallowing, the mingling of the sexes, in deference to the prevailing conservative Islamic and Judaic traditions. So one would find all the men's stores in one area, for example, and the women's in another. This was not Los Angeles, after all, where women actually had a legal right to use the men's restroom if the one designated to them was inaccessible or the waiting line was too long.

This particular shopping center had all the modern trappings, yet there was something ancient and subtly harsh which remained in it and which could be subtly discerned. True, the Middle East peace settlement enacted a few years ago was an unavoidable harbinger for social and economic change. It could not have been otherwise, already surpassing initial projections from the West for capital investment in the region. As everyone knows, where money is plentiful, ideas are not slow to follow, to develop, to find supporters.

The goal of private enterprise was profit, not conformity to tradition, necessarily, unless to do so would enhance financial gain. It was private enterprise and its rewards which paved the way, ultimately, for the absorption of Israel into the Arab Middle East, although not perhaps in the way it was initially envisioned. Yes, the predicted economic surge to the entire region occurred as planned, more or less, but much quicker and on a far grander scale. Evidence of prosperity was everywhere. Major hotel construction loomed at every boulevard. The main shopping thoroughfare in the area of Jebel Mukaber in Jerusalem was nothing short of a tourist's paradise-with a busy melange of coffeehouses, bookstores, fashionable boutiques, and eclectic restaurants to match the sophistication and vitality of a Champs Elysees or a Rodeo Drive.

Jerusalem was indeed proving itself irresistible to the world. Visitors flocked there by any available means, now that the borders were open. Crossing the border by air, boat, car, motorcycle, bicycle or just plain hitchhiking were acceptable methods. Who would have thought this possible five years ago, when the bickering and posturing of the Palestinians and the Israelis appeared endless and unsurmountable? In retrospect, the political holdouts against equal, distinct, yet contiguous countries for both peoples seemed anachronistic and myopic.

At the time of those historic negotiations, however, the U.S. State Department left nothing to chance. Agreements were reached on every outstanding issue of historic dissension: the shared use of the water supply, limits to immigration for both Palestinians and Israelis so as not to overwhelm the sensitive economy-painstakingly constructed and supported by the European Common Market, the United States, and Asia-and of paramount importance, the status of Jerusalem, which became the shared capital of both Israel and Palestine. Economic prosperity coupled with political expediency couched in sensitive language with the proper Arabic, Hebrew, and English nuances was ultimately the irresistible solution. Everyone knew that economic gain was a far better enticement to peace and regional cooperation than the forced military occupation of Palestinian land by an Israeli army.

Only five years had passed since that historic peace treaty, and already violence was rare and isolated in the region. The agreement did indeed appear to have been devised not only to insure stability but to create an omnific marketing and investment hub for the world. With animosity and violence seemingly a thing of the past, Israel and Palestine became each other's galvanizer. In a political rapprochement which would spawn dissertations in academic fields ranging from political science to feminist studies far into the 21st century, the successful settlement between these formerly virulent foes reminded many statesmen of a paradox-the enmity of two contentious peoples often resolving itself by even closer mingling, as opposed to mutual annihilation. Salvation may sometimes be found in one's nemesis, it was occasionally said. The more successful Palestine appeared to Israel, the more comfortable and secure the Israelis felt and the greater their own prosperity.

Reasons abounded for the world to support these political and economic breakthroughs, but none the more than the wish to finally rid itself of the massive guilt accumulated by years of military interference in the area. Finally, investment strategy succeeded where military prowess had failed. Financial coffers opened, succumbing to the lure of liberal tax laws for funding projects in both Palestine and Israel, all of which had become phenomenally successful in terms of return on investment. Once Jerusalem had quietly and elegantly taken its place in the world's consciousness as the dual capital for both Palestine and Israel, a thing unheard of in the old Likud government with its Eretz Israel obsession, solutions to ordinary political dilemmas seemed feasible, even Bosnia-Serbia-Croatia-Kosova, where the civil war continued to fester.

A neutral zone between Palestinian and Israeli Jerusalem had been created during the early stages of negotiation. Initially the function of that zone had been security, although later it had been transformed into a free trade zone. But now that the Palestinian/ Israeli borders had become as open as those between Canada and the United States, there were only a few circumstances which might change it from an almost imperceptible strip on the map to a forum for international debate. One of those had occurred a year ago.

About that time, an idealistic 18 year old youth by the name of Michael Bateson had arrived in Jerusalem. Michael reflected the wave of liberal thinking which had survived the alternate succession of liberal and conservative governments in the United States. There was no compelling reason for him to come to Jerusalem. He was not in school or working there. From a conservative point of view, he might easily have been characterized as a bum, a widely accepted euphemism for the unemployed and homeless, although that term was no longer politically correct.

Michael Bateson, however, did his share of existential self-questioning about values, ethics, and society. He obsessed continuously about why his parents divorced when he was only thirteen, at the threshold of his adolescence. A period known to be difficult and with the highest suicide rate of any life stage. He imagined that in some remote way, he might have been responsible. Yet, why couldn't they have waited to divorce, wait for him to acquire a semblance of maturity, for him to amass an arsenal of defenses for that final blow? Why destroy his only secure haven, flimsy though it was? The years following his parents' divorce were turbulent and emotionally catastrophic. He felt that his entire world had been torn asunder. The issue of something as mundane as "grade-point-average" became a moot point after he dropped out of school in his senior year at a prominent secondary school. His self-esteem plunged, his confidence waned and his personal and mental hygiene noticeably slipped.

Michael began to divert energy away from coping with the problems of living in a dysfunctional family to other activities and opportunities which presented themselves to him, capriciously or not, and which included people who accepted him unconditionally, like followers of rock bands and other fringe groups. He had played the guitar since third grade. "A successful musical autodidact," his mother was in the habit of proudly announcing. It was the one self-motivated activity that she and his father had supported.

Because of this innate musical ability, he was often asked to substitute for a band member and eventually became accepted as a valued itinerant addition to any number of struggling rock bands. One of these bands performed internationally and Michael considered it his great fortune to be the lead guitarist when the group traveled to Jerusalem for the Concert For Peace, an international commemoration of the Middle East Peace Agreement between Palestine and Israel. When the band left, he and many others, both musicians and tourists, decided to stay on, entranced with the hypnotic strangeness of that area of the world. For the first time in his young life he was able to completely relax into a noncommital mode of ambivalence about virtually everything-his country, his family, his friends. He no longer had to "be" anything-Protestant, American, from the East or West Coasts, in order to be accepted as an individual who was valued simply because he existed, because he was alive.

The inherent kindness of the people in the Middle East-both Jews and Arabs-aroused suspicion in him at first, until the sheer repetition of smiles and unsolicited greetings he received daily from perfect strangers won him over. How unlike New York! How unlike Los Angeles! He was adjusting, he thought, to a kinder world. The fact that he was neither employed nor in school yet, did not especially bother him. Productive, gainful employment was nothing more than acquiescence to a societal judgment about how people chose to use their time. Michael could not now be bothered with the morality of working or not working, let alone why his parents had made a mess of their lives. He could not change anything anyway and besides, there were many interesting diversional discoveries to be made in this world with which he was only becoming recently acquainted-as Michael Bateson, an individual.

Like selling things. He found, much to his delight and amusement, that he apparently had a talent for selling, for engaging the attention of perfect strangers in an enjoyable conversation, after which they had acquired one of his products, like the hand-embroidered jackets he bought for $30.00 and sold for $200.00.

Drugs unobtrusively slipped into his life. People he knew were engaged in the same issues, how to survive in a world back home which was not exactly hostile, yet not quite friendly either, and very different from the one he found himself in now. Some of them

ingested drugs, not for the goal which people commonly assumed-
excitement-but as a palliative, for the lack of ability to proceed in
life, for their angst. The emotional equilibrium drugs were able to
create was indeed artificial. Michael recognized that fact, but quickly
added such a state was better than having no equilibrium at all. It
was only a matter of time before Michael slid from the position of
rationalizing his friends' use of drugs to using them himself,
complete with the same excuses. He shared their prerequisites-
alienation from self, family, and country, and had no recognizable
goal.

In retrospect he would later link his soon to be changed fate to
the resilient climate of hysteria over drug use in the U.S., which
had spread like an airborne virus to the rest of the world. The
paranoia about drugs, addicts, and their proliferation into the very
heart of the American family, began in earnest with the annual
publication of a longitudinal study by the National Institutes of
Mental Health in the '80's. Such statistics prompted front-page
news stories every time elections were due, extolling the evils of
the lucrative drug-dealing business and the burgeoning addiction
of America's youth. The inevitable fear elicited in the public by
the government through the press was manipulated by politicians
every year, predictably, as stiffer crime bills were passed.

Congress could not be viewed as being "soft on drugs". America's
fascination with the drug culture was harnessed into votes for
politicians who made the building of federal prisons in the economic
and cultural wastelands of America a panacea for rural decay. Most
of the areas were the prisons were located were bereft of natural
resources, including physical beauty. The incarceration of people
for nonviolent behavior, for being mentally ill, for being homeless-
already less than optimum modes of existence, relatively speaking-
became a booming business.

Prisons proliferated and over-capacity conditions in newly built
facilities required the continuation of a policy of mandatory
minimum sentences. Long terms without parole needed to continue
in order to provide thousands of new inmates for the prisons which

had been built in deserted, underproductive areas all over the United States. Since the populations of rapists and murderers remained relatively stable, the ever-increasing number of convicted drug users provided a constant population flow into the prisons.

Soon nonviolent drug abusers outnumbered the violent criminals who in turn were often released early, so as to make more beds available for the now dominant prison population. Among those medical professionals who considered drug addiction a disease, the prospect of incarceration instead of treatment was an abomination. The role of prisons, it was generally agreed, had transformed from being rehabilitative to simply retributive. Victimless crimes, addictions, homelessness and mental illness were now managed by a method which originated out of the goal to protect society from dangerous people. Often one could find people in their early adulthood when they were imprisoned who would spend the rest of their lives behind bars because they used drugs. Congress condoned this practice though it did nothing to deter drug use in the population at large. Naturally, that was so, members of the medical establishment concurred, since an addiction is not cured by punishment. Drug use continued to rise among high school and college students. Prisons could not be built fast enough.

Juries handed down verdicts to drug abusers without realizing the harshness of the sentence they were assuring. Juror obey their instructions unflinchingly because they are basically good citizens trying to do the right thing. Most of them are unaware of how long mandatory minimum sentences are. Michael Bateson had several friends who were spending their lives vegetating in federal and states prisons. He thought of them every day.

Naive, reckless adolescents, a group of which Michael Bateson was surely a member, continued to experiment with mind altering substances. It was in the nature of youth to experiment. Some of them lost their lives to the criminal justice system because of this tendency, unfortunately. It was good for Michael to be out of the United States. He did not have to worry so much. It was too depressing to think about-so many friends and former classmates in prison.

True, he occasionally used drugs. They made him forget a lot of painful experiences he did not want to remember. They made him feel momentarily good. That was better than not ever feeling good about himself or about anything at all, for that matter. Particularly with LSD, his emotional problems seemed to diminish, ever so slightly, it seemed-after a short time spent integrating the experience and discussing it with others like himself. He was beginning to finally acknowledge, however, that he was the creator of his problems, not his divorced parents, not his country, not the world. In fact, he was noticing a minute sense of empathy toward his parents. Maturity adjusts attitudes in a much more complete and positive way than a prison ever will.

Once the necessity of blame was removed, he could regard his parents as the same frail human beings that he himself was, just as likely to make mistakes occasionally as to find success. The degree of hostility he had harbored against society and his own self was in fact diminishing, and he no longer experienced unpredictable and compulsive urges to destroy himself by whatever means available. One belief was unshakeable, though, and that was his view that the drug LSD as a psychological medication had as much potential to help people (or to be as misunderstood by them) as the serotonin-altering drug Prozac had been several years ago. And he realized the difference between the temporary use of a therapeutic agent and one which was used in the dangerously addictive way in which alcohol is often used instead of as a harmless component of and enhancer for social pleasure.

He believed himself to actually be a person who was anti-drugs, even though he condoned the medicinal uses of psychotropic drugs which were as yet unapproved by the Federal Drug Administration. (LSD was still in the testing stage before approval for use in the general populace by psychiatrists. Until then, people continued to be arrested for using it, despite whatever benign or therapeutic excuse they had to do so, and would nevertheless be considered criminals and treated accordingly.)

In fact, Michael's goal was to go to Switzerland to be part of a study group supervised by Dr. Peter Berman for the therapeutic uses of LSD. If accepted, he would join an elite group of carefully-selected volunteers from all over the world who would received LSD and psychotherapy for certain conditions amenable to such treatment, based on the Diagnostic and Statistical Manual (for mental disorders), Version VI. The last group which Dr. Berman had supervised enjoyed complete rehabilitation from depression and drug abuse. Michael's goal was to rely on himself for the enrollment and financing of the program. His perennially warring parents had no knowledge of where he was, anyway, or what he was doing, and that was fine with him. He had moved to Jerusalem and was self-sufficient. His independence was worth more than the comfort and safety which his parents might provide, and certainly the price for what they could give-the sacrifice of his individuality-was too high for him to pay.

Michael Bateson could not have known how soon his determination would be tested, when, on that particular afternoon, he decided to sell, from his collection, hopefully one or two embroidered jackets in the neutral trade zone between East and West Jerusalem. This particular month, in preparation for the winter holidays, had the entire Middle East, from Cairo to Amman to Jerusalem, and even to the newly resuscitated Beirut, inundated with pre-holiday tourists, mostly looking for pre-season bargains. Michael considered it a highly entertaining, as well as lucrative activity: the watching, the observing, of others, as they rummaged through his goods, some buying, some passing by. Engaging them in conversation, he found most of them gushingly, alternatively condescending or ingratiating, depending on their political sympathies, to the native population of Sabra Israelis or Palestinian Arabs.

Some of them had become textbook cases of culture shock. They exhibited weird, unpredictable behavior, like early schizophrenics do. There were cases which became legends and went on to be the subjects of T.V. documentaries and front-page tabloid news, such as the well-known cases of people assuming alternative personalities, alter-egos, other identities.

While it is strange enough to visit a psychiatric ward and experience the delusional state of a person who believes himself to be God, it is quite another thing to find a previously normal person, who was part of your tourist group, transformed before one's very eyes, into the personification of Moses or Jesus. The locals, of course, had gotten used to it. In fact, at peak tourist season it occasionally happened that there would appear more than one "Jesus" contending for attention on the same street, oblivious to the other's presence.

To the local shopkeepers, who had seen it all many times before, it was no more than an opportunity to transform, through the polished finesse of the seasoned Middle-Eastern businessman, the fashionable boutiques in the area. The "lost souls", as they came to be know in the Neutral Zone, became tourist attractions themselves. Articles began to be written about them. "Normal" tourists sought them out, camera at the ready. Academics were particularly curious, with their note-scribbling and tape recorders. Inevitably, two to three days later, a sensational report would appear in the Herald Tribune or The Jerusalem Post or the Palestinian Guardian or Al-Ahram about yet another sensational incident. Much later, a more discreet study might be published in one academic journal or another.

The psychological, political, and sociological consensus about this curious human behavior was that there are individuals whose lives, previous to visiting the Middle East, could be characterized as sheltered and sequestered, redolent with outdated views of what the world was like outside of their immediate environments. This orientation was consistent with the phenomenon of culture shock, but more complicated. What could not be grasped by these individuals was the in situ nature of contemporary culture-whose members quite possibly descended from ancestors who might have been part of the original crowd on the Via Dolorosa on a certain day in history when an innocent man was executed on Calgary.

His jury then was as insensitive to the truth and to the possible aftermath of their actions as juries are today. But one lost sight of that when standing on the very spot in Jerusalem where it all happened. It is not difficult to understand how a deeply religious person could become overwhelmed.

The more seasoned or perhaps jaded and objective traveler who had perhaps witnessed the mysteries of Karnak and the Church of the Holy Sepulcher, the Acropolis, the Great Wall of China and other wonders of the world, had found their way back to the World as It Is Right Now. In contrast, these naive travelers refused to believe what their senses were perceiving, that the present Israel and Palestine were inhabited by people who wore clothes very much like their own-seldom robes and sandals-and drove Mazdas and Audis and Subarus, instead of getting around by means of camels, donkeys, or horses, although those could surely be observed also. In all likelihood they spoke English as well as Arabic and possibly French, German or Italian as well.

In their staunch denial of the reality to which they traveled many thousands of miles to witness, they created instead an alternate world more resonant with Biblical times than with the 20th century. This hallucinatory state they accepted as real until they returned to saner mental harbors. Thus absorbed in narcissistic retrogression, they could easily conjure up a scene which for all purposes became reality for a time, in which they might be having coffee with John the Baptist instead of John the Barber, or suddenly encounter Moses while walking along the beach, or give a few coins to an indigent Mary Magdalene who was begging on the street.

It was a sort of temporary psychosis which was becoming commonplace in Jerusalem. When the level of dysfunction slipped to near-complete dissociation, as in the speaking of tongues and other exhibitionistic displays, it was time to remove the human spectacle from the premises. A consensual agreement between every shopkeeper, concierge and café owner in the Neutral Trade Zone and Dr. Yair Bar-In, an expert on altered psychological states provided for the swift removal by ambulance of these temporarily demented tourists. Dr. Bar-In was collecting data about such cases in order to substantiate a lucrative United Nations grant, purporting to study the mental health of tourists in so-called areas of former terrorist activity, which included Ireland and South Africa as well as Palestine and Israel.

Dr. Bar-In would miraculously appear at these scenes seemingly from nowhere with attendants in a discreetly unmarked ambulance and whisk the unfortunate person to Kfar Shom, a psychiatric hospital specializing in this unusual modern temporary mental illness which became known as The Jerusalem Syndrome. His techniques perfected, Dr. Bar-In retrieved the person, interviewed him or her, subjected the person to projective psychological testing, and put him or her on a standard regimen which included a short course of anti-delusional psychotropic medication and reality-adjustment psychotherapy. The rate of cure was almost 100%. Identities were reclaimed eventually and bizarre behavior disappeared in an alibi of amnesia. Honor regained, these unfortunate tourists, so ill-suited to exotica, returned home with the usual expected repertoire of sightseer stories and edited home movies.

But to the locals it was all wonderful grist for coffee-conversation.

"Moustapha, did you hear what happened on Jaffa Street yesterday?"

"No, Yuri, but it could not be better than what I saw today in Shlomo Square."

"With all due respect, my brother, nothing can beat *this* one! Here was a woman from Idaho-her name was "Clara". She thought she was Jesus' mother, Mary. After making a big scene and attracting a lot of people and money for the shopkeepers, she was eventually arrested and taken to Kfar Shom."

"Well, where else? Bar-In is making a fortune on these poor slobs. So what else is new?"

"Here's the funny twist. Clara, or Mary, was arrested as she was stuffing toys from the shelves of Ali's Toy Shoppe into a large cloth bag. When asked what was she doing, she said in reverent tones that she was collecting toys for Jesus to play with."

"He must gotten bored with the last set of junk from Ali's store," Moustapha said, his face reflecting the familiar sarcasm he felt when he heard of the preposterous behavior of many tourists.

"Crazy Americans," Moustapha continued, "what if WE went to Idaho, where they live, and pretended we were Richard Nixon."

"No, no, you're way off," Yuri retorted in obvious enjoyment. "Nixon is too recent. When you go to Idaho you must disguise yourself as Abraham Lincoln, now that would be more like it. But don't take my word for it! Here, read today's Jerusalem Post. It's all there on the front page. You know, these people aren't acting-they actually believe it. Thank goodness Bar-In is around. They might stay crazy were it not for him. What if they wanted to remain here? Anyway, what was your story?"

"I lose. I admit it," Moustapha conceded. "Mine is far less interesting. As God is my witness, a man from a city called "Looey-ville", Kentucky, locked himself up in the lion's cage at the Jerusalem Zoo and could not be persuaded to come out. He was ranting and raving."

"Don't tell me," Yuri laughed, "he called himself Daniel, right?"

Elsewhere in the city, Michael Bateson wondered what this particular day would bring. The unpredictability of life in Jerusalem was its most fascinating aspect. You never knew whom you might encounter in town or in the Neutral Trade Zone. Michael clung to a superstitious belief that everyone must pass through Jerusalem at some point during their lives. This week, for example, his old friend Wally, from rock concert days, had suddenly surfaced in Tel Aviv, en route to Italy. They shared a room and stories together. Michael had not seen Wally in two years and was anxious to hear what was going on in the States-politically and culturally-since he had left.

Wally, a balding, overweight, 35 year old ex-hippy from Madison, Wisconsin, lead a vagabond life. Lost between cultures, he had not yet agreed to an acceptable identity with which he might live out the rest of his life. He might never find that identity and Michael shuddered to contemplate the possibility of his ever becoming a nonentity like Wally, permanently fixed in an outdated lifestyle, unable to adjust to new opportunities and challenges, unable to change. Michael decided that after visiting Switzerland and completing the rehabilitation program with the celebrated Dr. Berman, he would make a serious attempt to organize his life into a coherent plan directed toward some reasonable goal.

Wally's decadence and unrecognized obsolescence was a strong predictor of the fate awaiting Michael should he not adjust the direction of his life. He knew, and Wally admitted, that he was still heavily involved in using LSD, but worse, had even begun selling it in order to finance his travels around the world. Michael, appalled by the direction his friend's life had taken, said nothing, but recognized in himself a strong urge to distance himself from the Wallys of this world, who, in his opinion, were the ones who would be spending 20 years behind bars alongside some students who used LSD at a party.

It seemed that Wally was not in the least deterred by the stiff sentences which were being given to drug offenders. Michael even wondered if Wally was aware that in some Third World countries, even harsher penalties than those that existed in the U.S. were practiced, like caning and beheading. There, one was literally risking one's life for something that might be only a misdemeanor in the United States, where the "plea-bargain" device for lowering sentences by informing on others to the government was one way one could get around a mandatory minimum sentence.

Wally remained headstrong and Michael reticent. Wally stated, in his bombastic manner, that LSD was the drug of the world. It commanded excellent prices, was simple to be transported even in tissue paper and its dealers, like dealers on other drugs, were relatively safe from prosecution. It was the users and small time sellers, the "suckers", Wally called them, who got the stiff sentences. The dealers knew exactly how to work the game of plea-bargaining.

To maintain one's innocence, in other words, was foolhardy. It was insane. You could never win and Wally was no fool. He took no chances. He transported the drug in sugar cubes or blotter papers in his backpack, or through the post office or air freight. For a person like Wally, undistinguished intellectually, academically, or personally, the only route to some sort of success, renown and friends, was through illegal activities. He had nothing to offer of any value in the straight, drug-free world, or so he thought.

Despite these basic differences, Michael still enjoyed Wally's company. His off-beat sense of humor and his independent nature were appealing, if deceiving. They stayed up until the early hours of the next day reminiscing and laughing about old times and old friends. Yet, Michael awoke only a few hours later, stuffing several embroidered jackets from Guatemala into his backpack, which he intended to sell in the Neutral Trade Zone in Jerusalem this afternoon. Then he quietly left, glancing back at this old friend Wally, the '60's throwback, still sleeping soundly. Michael expected to have a thoroughly satisfying and enriching day as he walked against an unusually strong wind toward the shopping district where he would set up his stall.

CHAPTER TWO

Washington

"If a crime with international overtones were to be committed at this moment in those two vulnerable countries, that is, our traditional ally, Israel, and our new-found friend, the fragile state of Palestine," the State Department's main speaker, a political scientist from Princeton, read from his notes, "political urges which had been repressed, and I stress, 'forcibly yet sensitively', with due respect to the indigenous cultures, by the Western peace-desiring consortium, would now be unleashed, with disastrous ripple effects on the entire world. Politics in the Middle East has traditionally, for many reasons, had a tremendous impact on almost every country I can think of. Certainly, the more vulnerable ones would be those just emerging from their own crises, such as South Africa. With the democratic government established by Nelson Mandela, and of course with apartheid dismantled, the former Soviet Union's intentions remain unpredictable in the region. Their reactions and our counter-reactions would unleash political energies with unpredictable consequences that would best be kept subdued."

This dire-sounding warning evoked much comment in the audience which had been assembled at short notice in Washington for a dinner commemorating the Palestinian-Israeli Peace Treaty. Not the least of these was Jonathon Miracle, a liberal, middle-aged attorney from Los Angeles, who was amused at having been invited in the first place, by the State Department. Except for the fact this his specialty was international criminal law, he could see nor reason why he had been included. Those doubts aside, he found himself agreeing with the speaker in many ways. Certainly since the dismantling of the Soviet Union and the destruction of Yugoslavia, the one success story in modern politics outside of South Africa, was the Palestine/Israel accord.

Those two still somewhat volatile states had, since the Treaty, become the embodiment of hope for a troubled world. It was certainly true that everything the United States had worked for since the peace talks were initiated in 1991 would be in jeopardy, should a political scandal develop. The source of direction for that treaty had been the pragmatic philosophy of statesmen like James Baker, who proceeded with dedicated energy to concretize his long-held belief that the mutual acceptance of Israel and its Arab neighbors could only be achieved through economic persuasion.

The secretive 1992 Madrid peace talks which he helped to devise were the springboard for the more public, more political negotiations between the Middle East warring factions which took place in Washington. By the time the journalists and television anchormen had assembled there, the difficult points of dissension had already been buried and a new agenda established. It only needed public announcements and hand shakes on the White House lawn, duly recorded by the Press, to acknowledge to the world that a new politic in the Middle East had evolved.

Part of the political baggage left behind in this new era was Israel's traditional and outdated policy of annexation of captured Palestinian or Lebanese land, ostensibly justified for its security needs. It had at long last been recognized, in part because of the inability to subdue a population by force, that when an individual prefers death to political subjugation, no amount of land can protect a people who value life above political compromise, not realizing that through political agreement life is preserved the most.

The Madrid meetings signaled a paradigm shift in the thinking of the policy-makers of all the countries involved which had been grappling with one aborted plan after another, based on the old mentality that military might makes right, as if it were an unassailable truth. The average American, so admiring of military technological superiority, and so delighted to see it in action particularly in far away places and not in their own back yard, had no understanding of the ideological struggles behind the decades-long conflict.

To them, whoever had more guns and bombs was the side they would bet on and vote more money for. American public opinion, as most educated Europeans already knew, was aroused and manipulated by a display of power. Weapons and the technology which supported them were key in the global struggle, a.k.a., political sport-the U.S. team vs. the Other team. The country with the most weapons would win. But the rules had changed, somewhere between the historic time when pride and dignity mattered and the computer age, where the funding and technology (or smart money) were sine qua non. Profit was an excellent resolver of conflict.

If smart money backed economic investment instead of the traditional military solution as a means to control other countries, it would be hard to find a middle-class American who could not understand that. The result of monetary enrichment of the U.S. was highly valued, even though no one would admit that. Never before in fact had the Guns-or-Butter argument been so clearly delineated, so candidly presented and so successful, with the "butter" going to the country which had formerly been targeted for persuasion by force.

The rules of political strategy had slowly changed, so that symbolic weapons of economic investment, which gave people reasons to live and prosper, replaced actual weapons of destruction, where one's choices were limited to only two: death or capitulation and victory (followed by financial aid to the vanquished). By opening the Madrid committees to the European community and Japan, James Baker had brilliantly enlarged the circle of brokers for peace, reducing the power of any one single country to dominate the playing field. It was clear to the participants in Madrid that Israel would not drown by being forced into the sea by Arab radicals, but by its own doing instead, by suffocating by inflation and a bankrupt economy heavily dependent on U.S. aid at a time when Americans were turning inward toward their own social problems and fiscal needs.

The cognoscenti, among whom Jonathon Miracle considered himself, recognized quite early in those negotiations that the future of the Middle East had been decided in Madrid. The issues of past violence which riveted the public could be debated in Washington and aired via CNN all over the world until such time as Madrid succeeded. Economic cooperation between all Middle East countries and now Israel-but as an integral part this time, not in its self-imposed long-time role of Hated Persecutor of Palestinians. The establishment of a free trade zone between itself and Palestine funded by a newly-formed bank for Middle Eastern Development was proof that sensible planning could work, despite the heated polemic. At long last, that one giant step into modernity was at the brink of being taken by a major part of the Third World, and Jonathon, like most people, breathed a sigh of relief. Prosperity had won. Fear and Terror had lost.

"We can all recall," the Princeton professor continued, "when in 1992 the United States federal deficit was $314 billion. The Clinton administration recognized that a deficit of this size was consuming savings and private investment while simultaneously raising the cost of borrowing. That could only mean one dreaded result as far as Israel was concerned: less money in the form of grants and interest-free loans. And because supply-side economics had failed, the new administration was faced with an enormous economic challenge: to limit foreign aid while honoring its economic promises at the peace table.

"Palestine and Israel, having done their part by agreeing to a permanent peace and mutual recognition, waited hopefully for the funds to pour in. Could the U.S. afford it? Could we, in effect, have our cake and eat it too?"

"These things take time, and unfortunately we didn't have a lot of that. The plan was to stimulate investment abroad, particularly in the new area of Palestine. Then, the accrued corporate taxes from those profitable investments could be applied back home to the accumulated national debt. If, as everyone suspected would be the case, which has proven to be true, that profits would be so outstanding that the tax burden on international companies would be negligible, it would be a sound strategy. It was and still is a 'win-win' situation. What helped us immensely was the fact that most of the Palestinian economic team were academically degreed in the United States at some of our most prestigious institutions, so they understood very clearly how our policies are shaped.

"That their sense of philosophy was more influenced by the centrist economists here, such as Harvard's Benjamin Friedman, instead of the standard Marxist heroes of the Third World, made dealing with them much more pleasant than with Cuba, for example. To show our appreciation, we granted tax-free status for Palestinian Bonds, as we have long done for Israel, and we were not disappointed by our generosity. The overwhelming diasphoric Palestinian community gave to the fledgling state far beyond our expectations. We have made all the right moves so far." The professor, growing slightly hoarse, paused briefly to sip some ice water.

"But we're not out of danger yet," he continued. "Old animosities die hard and here at the State Department that fact is recognized more than perhaps in Palestine and Israel itself. Should those animosities be aroused once again, the fragile peace so painstakingly achieved just a few short years ago could evaporate into thin air, with Yugoslavian-Bosnian-Kosovian like consequences. The two Semitic entities have been enemies for longer than they have been friends, and we can't take a short-lived peace for granted. Strong, though subdued, political divisions remain. The Likud religious Israeli conservatives and their counterparts on the other side, the Hamas people, are still alive and kicking, the secular-liberal Palestinians and the Israeli Meretz Party trying to maintain a precarious balance amongst themselves.

"The more radical fringe groups on both sides are perfectly capable of precipitating a crisis over the smallest incident at any time, with tragic consequences. There is intra-State as well as inter-State tension and unresolved issues and feelings of entitlement and zealots. The zealots are particularly embarrassing troublemakers. There are conservative Jews who believe in risking their lives confronting the Army in an effort to have the government ban all transportation on the Sabbath because it is sacrilegious. Then they would be armed with the law to force all Israeli citizens, even the non-Jewish ones to comply with their religious obsessions. There is no lack of promiscuous altruists, either, who are capable of destroying the whole place agreement to satisfy their myopic causes. Political mines cover the earth, but are surely more concentrated in the area we call the Middle East. I am here to tell all of you that the interest of the United States is to preserve the present peace between the new Palestinian state and Israel-*by all means.*"

Resounding applause followed. Handshakes. The Press photographed for ten constant minutes. "Promiscuous altruists, indeed!" someone to the left of Jonathon Miracle stated.

"What?"

"The damned promiscuous altruists he was mentioning. They aren't happy unless they are destroying and protesting in the name of their 'causes'". No one wants to think about the intangibles. What about respect for the individual cultures? Are we going to see in the immediate future American fast-food chains on every block in West Jerusalem? Will the American Colony become a Hotel Intercontinental? Now, that is a plan worth fighting against! You've been there, haven't you? Oh, sorry, I don't believe we've met. I'm a cultural ecologist . . ."

"A what? Oh, how interesting. I'm Jonathon . . ."

"Jonathon Miracle?" A Senate aide interrupted. "I have an urgent message for you, sir."

Jonathon was overjoyed at an excuse to avoid this inflated academic, whose cultural ecology was a metaphor for anthropology, a subject he had long considered hopelessly peripheral to reality.

"Thank you," he responded as he quickly arose from his seat, nodding without looking at the gentleman beside him.

"Miracle. Now that's an odd name," the now abandoned cultural ecologist was left to contemplate.

Not looking at the message itself, Jonathon left the hall in search of a quiet corner with a telephone. Why was he here, anyway? Did someone need *his* brand of promiscuous altruism? Word was out that the State Department was looking for a legal expert on international affairs for a particular assignment. Since Jonathon's name was often in the news lately because of his pro-bono work in defending incarcerated youths (one of whom was his own brother, who had been convicted of smuggling drugs internationally), he was not totally surprised to receive an invitation to the dinner he was now attending. It was a good opener. Now, Jonathon hastened to make that phone call and find out what was really behind the invitation.

In the few moments it took to dial the number neatly written on the paper the senate aide had given him, he remembered the turmoil years ago, when he had stood against the mighty federal government and their arbitrary laws . . .and won. Jonathon had changed his career from medicine to law, switching in his second year of medical school. His brother's case was his first. And because of these efforts, his brother had his sentence-based on a contrived charge of drug conspiracy-reduced from 20 to 5 years, and eventually won clemency and a pardon.

"You're good, Miracle. Someone to keep in mind," said his adversary, a seasoned federal attorney who had since been his opponent many times in court.

It had also cost him his marriage, thought Jonathon ironically. Yet, had his wife been in love with him as a person and not as a symbol of future success, the marriage would not have foundered, he was convinced. Then again, he might not have realized until years later that he had married the wrong woman. His conclusion? That promiscuous altruists may be better off remaining single. His wife had left him because he stood by his brother and ultimately by his own goals, which entailed abandoning medical school for law school. Her future was unilaterally defined as one path and one path only, as success for herself in the role of wife of a physician. She could not adapt to the changing forces emerging within him, nor to the challenges of life. She was completely devoid of courage, dexterity, and imagination. Still, he had loved her and his sadness at losing her would persist for his entire life. The government, with its direction defined by corruption and the popular vote, was not a standard by which to live a life of principle. His reverie was interrupted by the animated voice on the other end of the phone.

"This is a matter of extreme urgency, Mr. Miracle. It is a case which needs the utmost tact, a thorough knowledge of international and domestic laws regarding drug trafficking."

"Which you already know I have because of my brother's case."

"Precisely. Look at this way, Mr. Miracle, we at the Central Intelligence Agency have been watching. We were impressed. Your brother is now free. You faced very difficult hurdles. It didn't happen by accident. We need your talents. It's an opportunity to even the score in a case in which we both have deep interest."

"Really. What is that?"

"Well, to be quite frank, Mr. Miracle, the case if very much like your brother's. Your client will almost be assured of an acquittal. As you heard tonight, our government does not want any scandals to erupt in the Middle East regarding sensitive issues. I'm sure you were impressed with what the speaker said this evening, a man of great distinction whom we arranged to come here."

"Definitely, but where's my challenge, if the case is already assured of an acquittal."

"We need you to smooth things out, to say things diplomatically. I might point out that there is always the chance that the fundamentalist way of handling crimes like this in that area of the world, namely, by beheading or hanging, is a dangerous possibility. We must avoid that. We must tie this case up early and quickly, and the less news coverage the better."

Jonathon's vulnerabilities were touched. The CIA agents were clever, they had done their homework. Of course, they were from the PSYCOPS Department, and so were well-trained in the manipulation of minds and emotions.

"Perhaps you would like to hear about the accused. He's nineteen years old, a produce of a divorced home, dismissed from school, highly intelligent, but sort of a vagabond."

"I'll take the case, PSYCOPS. Send me everything I need, including first class tickets to Jerusalem," Jonathon heard himself announcing. It felt good to dictate to the CIA.

Now, only a few hours later, Jonathon Miracle was on a flight to Tel Aviv, getting used to his new title, "Special U.S. Counsel" in the Israel-Palestine v. Bateson case. He was amazed at the incredible speed with which arrangements were made. "That's power for you," he thought. Then he smiled at his own stupidity. It had probably all been pre-arranged weeks ago. He was like the unsuspecting prey blundering into the master spider's web. "Well, they may be getting what they want, the clever bastards," Jonathon thought, "but I will find something of interest in this for me."

He decided to familiarize himself with the case immediately, reaching for his briefcase, given the fact that he had an eleven hour flight ahead of him. He still felt a gnawing humiliation at having been second-guessed and controlled by the CIA, but he chose to allow his logic to squelch his hubris. He had, after all, accepted the assignment. Now, emotions aside, he had to give it his best effort.

Opening the brief summarizing the case of Israel-Palestine v. Bateson, Jonathon forced himself to concentrate solely on the issue before him and to block out all residual emotional contaminants. One of our young American citizens was in trouble in the Middle East. Some sort of trumped-up drug charge in Jerusalem. The conservative radicals in both Israel and Palestine had seized upon the issue as a means of advancing their causes, a familiar tactic to gain national attention. The charges themselves should have been dismissed immediately, given the lack of evidence directly incriminating Michael Bateson. But someone had informed the Press of a possible international cover up, and a cause celebre was born.

Something newsworthy has at last surfaced in the Middle East, since the recent dearth of suicide attacks on Israelis and the cold-blooded murders of Palestinians by Israelis. Those incidents, tragic though they were, were becoming rare. But the Press, as ever, sought sensationalism.

It seemed that Michael Bateson, an adolescent visiting Jerusalem without his parents, had decided to sell a small amount of LSD. Nothing strange about that. Since the Swiss government had reopened LSD research at the Association of Physicians for Psychedelic Therapy in Zurich, the drug had regained tremendous popularity in psychotherapeutic circles throughout the world. The growing acceptance of the medical profession of the therapeutic potential of the drug played a large part in the reduction of the extraordinarily long sentences for LSD offenses in the United States. In fact, as the CIA well knew, that was one reason for Jonathon's success in his own brother's case several years ago.

Unfortunately, the Third World, in its zeal to clone themselves into replicas of the United States, was always at least a decade behind it, was itself years behind the more enlightened European countries. Naturally conservative and slow to legislate social reform, the Justices in the lagging countries were maddeningly cautious in their interpretations of anything progressive or new, be it regarding women or the ubiquitous nature of drug use.

In fact, much to Jonathon's amazement, the judges in Michael Bateson's case were using the same absurd table with which to calculate his sentence as was used in his own brother's trial. He had fought so hard to change the sentencing of human beings from being determined by a grid, where the x and the y axis meet, to the discretion of an objective yet compassionate judge. True, judges' sentences for similar crimes were still not uniform, but neither were the circumstances of human beings. By the logic of mandatory minimum sentencing's grid formula, naive students and seasoned drug dealers would receive the same sentence, despite their vastly different circumstances..

But of course it didn't work out that way, since the wizened dealers had ample funds to hire the best attorneys, they were released in a matter of hours. The unfortunate young people, however, whose families could not often afford the minimum of $50,000 required, even for a mediocre attorney to defend their son or daughter, often were assigned overworked, underpaid, and unfortunately, all too often, incompetent attorneys. Jonathon raised that point over and over again to drug reform opponents, who kept thinking, like a mantra, "zero tolerance, zero tolerance." What they were really expressing without realizing it is their wish for "zero survivors" of the War on Drugs.

The unsung heroes became those few, brave family members who organized themselves to fight the system through volunteer organizations, such as the one in Washington which called itself F.A.M.M., for "Families Against Mandatory Minimums"; or another one in California, F.A.C.T.S., for "Families Against California's Three Strikes". Three Strikes was a particularly virulent form of mandatory minimum law, sentencing the offender for 25 years to life for a third offense. It seemed to escape the minds of supporters of Three Strikes and other similar drug laws at the state level, that a person was being sentenced according to a crime for which he had already been punished, and that there was something ethically and legally wrong with that action.

Jonathon had the greatest respect for the unpaid volunteers of these grass-roots movements. They faced the ignorance and prejudice of the majority of Americans, who were manipulated and frightened by Congress and the Press into allowing the passage of outrageously unfair laws. If he could, Jonathon would devote the rest of his life to rehabilitation efforts of the incarcerated, such as education and job preparation. It didn't take much insight to realize that when a sentenced person was released after ten to twenty years, the world had changed in the interim, and the chance of the now-released offender's accommodating to what must appear as an alien environment, without training, preparation, or therapy, was practically nil.

Jonathon, in his battle for prisoners' rights, was often reminded of servicemen returning from Vietnam to a hostile American society which had nothing to offer them. In the state of California, where Jonathon lived, the number of homeless, jobless veterans was a disgrace. In both populations-inmates in prisons and veterans—individuals are removed from a rapidly-changing society where traditional jobs disappear and the rules for success dramatically change during their absence. They return as misfits.

The pain and disillusionment of these Americans at their inability to reintegrate was enduring. Still, in relative terms, what the convicted American drug offender could expect seemed far more humanitarian than what their counterparts might receive as punishment in third world countries such as Egypt. There, no rehabilitation is considered and the sentence itself could be much harsher than twenty years, perhaps life or worse.

Was it worth Jonathon's time and effort to save a young American caught up in some drug escapade? There was no question in Jonathon's mind, yet he felt vaguely weary, as though he had been fighting a futile battle against those in society who desired to condemn and to obliterate deviance from what it collectively defined as acceptable norms of behavior.

Jonathon found it just as ludicrous that the basic elements of the liberal American lifestyle were rapidly adopted by third world countries as well—utilitarian-type food on the run, hamburgers and fried chicken and pizza, the antipathy of the European palate. Jonathon was also amused to contemplate the tenacious stubbornness of these cultural differences. Which would win, the Hamburger or the Quiche Lorraine?

To force concentration on the Bateson case before sleep overtook him, somewhere over the Atlantic on his way to Tel Aviv, Jonathon abstained from the complimentary port or cognac after dinner, and had several cups of strong coffee instead. Then he examined the case in earnest.

Michael Bateson had been apprehended at the very dividing line between Israel and Palestine in the shared capital of Jerusalem. That fact precipitated unique legal problems which, in order be addressed, necessitated the immediate gathering of legal experts and judges from Palestine, Israel and the United States. It was impossible to deflect the Press from its attraction to a potentially sensational case: an American citizen living abroad, sentenced for selling drugs in a so-called "neutral trading zone" between two sovereign states, Israel and Palestine.

The witnesses for the prosecution had been an American tourist and an ultra-orthodox Jewish citizen. Not a very auspicious situation, Jonathon thought. Almost daily, the front page of *Jerusalem Post* was already devoted to some arcane aspect of the Bateson Drug Affair, as it became know across Europe.

Among the international groups, the consensus was that in order to save the young man's life, an American attorney for the appeal would be indispensable. Now that Jonathon Miracle had filled that role, it remained for him to fashion an argument which would prove irresistible, irrefutable, unassailable and perhaps somewhat sensational. Jonathon reasoned that since the media was looking for something to sensationalize about on its own, it would be better and safer for him to direct them to material which would serve a good cause once it was published.

That way, they wouldn't concentrate so much on the substantive issues, which they were likely to misinterpret anyway. The appeal would, after all, be instantly transmitted to the world at large. People had long since become accustomed to being entertained by the grand drama of a live hearing, since the Clarence Thomas and Anita Hill sensation and later by the trial of O. J. Simpson. The acquittal of nineteen year old Michael Bateson was supposedly already pre-arranged by the governments of Palestine, Israel and the United States. A deal had been made. Jonathon was a red herring. Jonathon would make the most of the situation.

What remained for Jonathon to do, then, was to seize the opportunity to expose an incident of blatant corruption, some insidious undertaking of the CIA, perhaps? Jonathon was not going to let this golden opportunity pass him by. On a lighter note, he enjoyed traveling and was in dire need of a vacation. One paid for by the Central Intelligence Agency was especially appealing. He felt smug.

About to fall asleep now, Jonathon reviewed the PSYCOPS part of the Bateson report from the CIA. Their reviews were always a little more interesting, a lot more human, given their psychological orientation, than the strictly legal interpretations. Jonathon was not disappointed. Apparently, the separation of Michael Bateson's parents a few years ago had been especially traumatic for Michael. For whatever reasons, some people withstand tragedy with hardly a hair out of place, seemingly, while others are permanently scarred. Michael displayed intense emotional instability and lapses in judgment as revealed in his letters to an uncle in Portland, Maine. At first he reveled in his freedom, describing in minute detail the pleasures of Jerusalem: great music, interesting girls, a fascinating history which confronted you at every turn, avant-garde theater, and wonderfully diverse food. Those kinds of letters continued for a while, after which the communication suddenly stopped.

Apparently Michael had decided to remain in Jerusalem for an indeterminate length of time, despite his parents' protestations. He had made friends with a group of wandering American and European youths who, in addition to being in the music business, were also apparently selling small quantities of drugs, particularly LSD. Jonathon could hardly believe the naivete of the youth, considering the fact that public and legal opinion in most countries would be strongly against them. Didn't they consider the consequences, he thought? But most youth were like that, oblivious to the danger they were creating for themselves. Sentences varied, but in general, they could be characterized as uniformly harsh, despite the age of the drug offender at the time of the crime. Jonathon found himself once again imagining an authority so obstinate in the belief of its moral certainty that it dismissed the value of repentance or rehabilitation. Such a criminal justice system doomed its citizens to a state of unredemption.

Unable to restrain himself from sleep any longer, Jonathon fell into one of those deep slumbers within which a dream seems more real than a stroll down Madison Avenue on a Monday morning. If he could have predicted his thoughts earlier he might have taken a sleeping pill, which would have obliterated the recall of the dream later. Too late. He was already in an oft-visited place, the interview room in the psychiatric unit of Block County Jail.

"Lola, this is Mr. M.," Dr. Larry blurted out in his customary, curt fashion.

"Hi, how're ya' doin'?" Lola, a plump white middle aged woman in baggy jeans with dyed blond hair and a strict looking face, queried.

"Fine. But please call me Jonathon."

"Oh no, Mr. M.", retorted Dr. Larry, "here, all the newcomers have to go through the initial stage, get it? the "Initial" stage! Your initial, "M". Anyway, it's a good way for so many staff that we have here in the jail to remember you quickly. Lola, will you show Mr. M. how we do interviews around here? He's a 2nd year medical student and I don't think they taught him anything about interviewing. Would you mind? You can start anywhere you like."

"Well, all right, Dr. Larry," Lola said unenthusiastically, her voice drifting off into a bored whine. She hated having to break new people in, although Mr. M. was a medical student and he was male, not too bad-looking. She would be the first person to introduce him to the others. That was a plus for her. It made her feel important, like she knew people and things that others did not.

"Okay, let's start with the Welcome Area," Lola shuffled along in front of Jonathon toward the elevators. She lit up a Parliament filter cigarette and left it dangling on her lip.

"The Welcome Area?"

"Yeah. We call it that because that's where people go when they're brought here after being arrested on the street. They have to be interviewed and medically examined, the whole bit. If they have anything mental in their past, they come up here."

"Oh."

"I'll leave you here in good hands. Come back upstairs after lunch" said Lola as she ushered Jonathon into a cavernous basement-type room flanked by large open cells filled with prisoners.

"They're called detainees, not prisoners," Lola said, as if reading his mind.

"And one more thing, no smoking is allowed on the compound" she said unsmilingly as she took a deep drag on her Parliament filter. "See, they can't pay their bail, that's why they're here. They're not supposed to be guilty of anything. They haven't had a trial or a plea-bargain yet. So they're stuck here. Of course some people don't get bail. That's the deal."

"Why wouldn't they get bail?"

"Because if you murder someone, you don't get bail," Lola said in a bored-sounding monotone. Lola turned on her heel leaving Jonathon in a cloud of cigarette smoke. The many officers in the Welcome Area didn't seem to notice that she was smoking. Some of them were smoking themselves. Jonathon found his way to the cramped and filthy office of the Psychologist in charge, Dr. Z., a short, blond American women dressed in skin-tight jeans and T shirt, giving the appearance of contrived adolescence.

"Have a seat," she said, pointing to a metal frame chair with the vinyl seat cushion torn and its stuffing sticking out. "So you're a medical student. Why are you here?"

"Because I'm interested in forensic psychiatry. When this fellowship became available, I applied and was accepted."

"No! I don't mean *that*. I mean *WHY* are you here, the real *why?*"

For some reason, Jonathon, who did not like probing by perfect strangers, heard himself disclosing very intimate information to this perky, no-nonsense woman who wanted to get at people's motives.

"Well, I . . .my brother . . .is serving a long mandatory minimum sentence for a drug offense and is incarcerated in the federal system. I wanted to see for myself what he might be going through, so that I could understand, so that I could see if he could survive it, what he was facing, etc."

"Well, we all have our reasons," Dr. Z. hummed, unimpressed. "How long did he get?"

"Twenty years."

"How old was he when sentenced?"

"Eighteen."

"Gees," Dr. Z. looked slightly empathetic.

Just then they were interrupted by two officers. That was fortunate, because Jonathon was already regretting confiding in Dr. Z.

"Got a backdoor for you, doc," one of the burly black officers stated.

"Don't call them 'guards', they hate that," Lola had warned him. The officers nudged a middle-aged black woman in a beige jail uniform into the office. She was handcuffed and had shackles on her ankles. Jonathon wondered why that was necessary. Certainly she wasn't going to try to escape in the belly of a jail!

Dr. Z. turned toward the woman. "Sit down, " she ordered.

The officers left the small office and lingered around outside in the hall, lighting up cigarettes.

"Why are you here?" Dr. Z. reiterated what must be sort of a mantra with her, Jonathon thought.

"I can't stand it no more, doc. I keep thinking about what happened and then I start crying. I can't take it anymore. I need some help."

"Do you feel like killing yourself?" Dr. Z. asked unemotionally.

"Oh yeah, I do."

"How would you do that?"

"Oh, I might use a light bulb," the inmate said nonchalantly, as if she were talking about fixing a broken appliance.

Suddenly Dr. Z. erupted. "Get out of here, you mother-fucker! You heard what I said! Get up off your ass and get out of my office. Go back to where you came from. You ain't got nothin' comin'".

The officers looked unimpressed. Jonathon said nothing, betraying none of the astonishment he was feeling.

"But doc, I . . ." the inmate attempted to continue.

"SHUT UP, YOU SON OF A BITCH AND GET OUT OF HERE. OFFICERS!"

The officers stepped in immediately and dragged off the hapless women, who was sobbing back to wherever she came from.

"Now," Dr. Z. calmly turned toward Jonathon, "can YOU do that?"

Ignoring the challenge, Jonathon asked, "what is her charge?"

"Involuntary manslaughter. She was high on cocaine and drunk on whiskey and she hanged her grandson." Dr. Z. didn't bother to explain further as she took a phone call. She scribbled "Go to lunch now" on a piece of envelope and slid it to Jonathon.

Not knowing where lunch could be had and still in somewhat of a state of shock after witnessing the scene in Dr. Z's office, Jonathon found himself alone in a long poorly lit tunnel. He walked for about 5 minutes and then at a turn, came across a well-dressed young black woman in the hall leading back up to the Psychiatric Unit, or P.U. for short. He asked her where he could have lunch.

"Go through the 2 tunnels in front of you, one right after the other, then through the unguarded iron gate, then up the stairs, and you'll see it. It's the employee cafeteria. Meals are free, but watch out for the cockroaches and rats."

Jonathon turned and looked at the woman to see if she were joking, but she had a somber look on her face. "I'm serious, she said. I don't eat there any more because of an incident which happened to me . . .Oh, never mind, I warned you."

Making his way through the second tunnel, Jonathon heard steps of several people coming his way around a bend ahead. Suddenly eight white officers came upon him walking briskly by. In their midst was a black man, his hands cuffed behind him and his face bleeding. He glanced at Jonathon, said nothing, then continued looking forward and kept marching.

Jonathon did not have much of an appetite by the time he finally reached the cafeteria. That series of tunnel-walking was unsettling, not only because of the encounter with the bleeding inmate. There were not many people in the tunnels and you could walk for a long time without seeing or hearing anyone else. It must not have been the most popular route to the main building where the cafeteria was housed. It made Jonathon a little uneasy thinking about it.

After lunch, Jonathon went back to the P.U. Unit and was greeted by a tall, lanky black female officer with a hint of American Indian features.

"I hear you're the new doc on PU," she said. "Hi, I'm Officer Merlin."

"Hi, I'm Mr . . ."

Before Jonathon could finish, a loud banging was heard coming from one of the rooms where the detainees were confined. Officer Merlin said, "Excuse me," turned sharply and, with long strides, reached the door where the noise was emanating from. It had a large shatterproof window on it. Jonathon saw an obese black woman, naked from the waist up, pressing her chest against the glass and staring right at Jonathon with unblinking wide eyes.

"I'm warning you, Mary," Officer Merlin, nonplused, said sternly. "Get back away from the door and put your shirt back on. We're not interested in looking at those flapjacks, hear?"

Officer Merlin turned back to Jonathon. "How do you like it here so far?"

Without waiting for an answer, she added, "Oh, and by the way, any of the chicks around here try anything like that again, which they probably will, you being male and all, you just turn around the other way, because you're not supposed to see that."

Lola reappeared from somewhere behind Jonathon. "I hope you didn't take more than an hour for lunch," she stated.

"Hey, Merlin," Lola continued, a little more upbeat. Merlin looked up from her desk, stationed in front of the patient-inmate Mary's door. "Who should we use as a guinea pig for the doc here to cut his teeth on?"

Merlin erupted in raucous laughter. "We have our pick here, don't we? How about . . .? Well, look behind you, our prayer's have been answered."

Lola and Jonathon turned around. Two male officers had just walked through the double doors of the PU and were advancing at a medium pace down the long, cell-lined hall towards them.

"One on the new, aren't you lucky," said Lola.

Merlin got up and took the large yellow envelope from the officers, exchanged a couple of jokes and then took the new inmate, a disheveled, middle-aged, thin white woman with long stringy hair, into a vacant room.

"Take your clothes off. Turn around. Squat. Cough." Merlin dictated military-style while she put on a pair of white latex gloves.

"Come on over here, doc," Lola said while turning around. "You're not supposed to watch because you're male." Lola's eyebrows arched up and down a couple of times and a seductive smile slowly blossomed on her face. "Let's go over to the men's side while Merlin does the paperwork on this babe."

The male PU mirrored the female unit in every detail except that it was on the opposite side of the building. A young woman was interviewing a Hispanic male inmate off to the side of the large day room. Lola thought it would be a good idea to sit in. They pulled up their chairs. Neither the inmate nor the interviewer seemed to notice.

"Do you feel suicidal right now?" The interviewer asked.

"Yeah."

"Are you hearing voices?"

"Yeah."

"Do you feel like hurting yourself?"

"Yeah. Like I told you, I'm going to do it first chance I get."

"Okay Officer" We've got to put this one down."

Two officers lumbered over. The nurse at the desk nonchalantly pulled open a drawer and lifted out a set of leather straps. The other inmates were all at their windows, watching.

"Okay, buddy, let's go," one of the officers said in a flat tone.

"Can I call my mother first?" the inmate asked plaintively. He looked so despondent, so desperate, tearful, afraid.

The officers looked at the interviewer.

"Sure, why not." She answered.

"Jana, this is Mr. M.," Lola stated. "He's a med student, going to be with us about a year."

"Hi. What do you think of this place so far?" Jana asked.

"Hi. Well, it's really interesting."

"That's true, and you'll see things here that you have never seen in your life before and will never see again," she confided.

"How long have you worked here?" Jonathon asked.

"About 5 years. I have a psych degree. I thought that I would go on to graduate school, but the pay here is so good, and I . . .I guess I kind of got used to the money, you know? Anyway, maybe we can have lunch sometime. Right now I've got a ton of new patients to see."

"Okay, and thanks," Jonathon said, happy to have at last met a colleague in the field.

Lola was irritated and motioned for him to follow her.

"She's a royal bitch, that one," she said.

"Oh?"

"Yeah. She's real high falutin', thinks she's some kind of genius or something. She's no better than any of the other Psych Techs around here. But she puts on airs."

Lola, Jonathon and the new female inmate, now in a beige uniform with a very low V-neck, were in an interview room together. Jonathon couldn't help noticing the woman's cleavage. She seemed unconcerned. When their eyes met, she looked defiant and angry.

"Let's get this over with right away. I've got better things to do, " she grumbled.

"Oh, a smart ass!" Lola said wryly. "You'd better cooperate because you know what we do with smart asses around here?"

"Are you threatening me? I've got a master's degree! You can't talk to me like that! I've got rights."

"Uh-huh," drawled Lola, "I've heard that one before. Officer!"

Merlin appeared out of nowhere.

"Tell this bitch all about this place."

"Well," Merlin began, "we didn't invite you here, see? This is like, our home, not yours, and so that makes you our guest. And if we don't like our guests' behavior, then you ain't gonna like ours. It's as simple as that."

"You're threatening me again! I'm going to call my lawyer!" the inmate shouted.

"Oh, shut up," Lola yawned, "if you had a lawyer, you would have already been out of here. How come you can't pay your $100 bail?"

The inmate was enraged. Merlin straightened up.

"Just answer the questions, okay? Make it easier on all of us," she said quietly.

"What questions? All I've been hearing are insults and threats."

"Like, are you hearing voices?" Lola asked.

"No, are you?"

"Do you feel like killing yourself right now?"

"No, do you?"

"Do you feel that people are out to get you?"

"Isn't it obvious?"

"Have you ever seen a psychiatrist, taken psychiatric medication, or stayed in a psychiatric hospital?" Lola continued, glancing down at the form she was checking off.

"No comment," the inmate replied.

"Okay, Merlin, take her away. We're done," Lola declared. "What a bitch, huh?"

"I imagine she wasn't typical," Jonathon ventured.

Lola had a smirk on her face when she said, "You and Jana are going to get along just fine."

The next day Jonathon, with a handful of interview forms went to the Men's PU as assigned by Lola before she left to play pool and have a few cigarettes. Jonathon refused the invitation to join her and a few others. He spent the next 2 hours sitting and chatting with Officer Merlin because there was nothing else for him to do.

"See, we're on lock-down. You can't talk to nobody and they can't come out. Aren't you lucky? You'll find a lot of cards and checker sets for the Psych Staff in the top drawer over there," Merlin laughed. "That's what you all do when we're on lock-down."

"Am I supposed to know what that means?" Jonathon retorted, good naturedly, as he was beginning to like Officer Merlin.

"If the count is off, if we're short on officers, or something's been found, we go on lock-down," she replied.

"Like..?"

"Like drugs or a shank. Once in a while, someone escapes, but they usually don't get too far. It's usually a guy and he always goes to the girl friend's house if he gets that far. And that's the first place they look."

"Lock-down. Is that why Lola went to play pool with some of the others, because there's nothing much to do?"

"Hell, no. She plays pool every afternoon with her buddies, from 2 to 4 P.M. on County time, whether it's lock-down or not."

"You must be kidding. I thought maybe today was an exception."

"No it ain't. A lot of people get away with a lot of shit around here."

"Doesn't Dr. Larry ever notice?"

"Sure he does. We all do. But they don't care, get it? It's as simple as that."

Jana was waiting in the men's unit when Jonathon arrived. There was a roomful of about 6 male inmates seated in a circle. Jana said it was group therapy time.

"Have you ever done a group before?" she asked.

"No, actually, I can't say that I have. I'm a medical student, don't forget. I spend most of my time studying anatomy books and very little time with living, breathing patients. That's why it's such a treat for me to be here."

"Well, don't get carried away now. We're going to try to do a group therapy session today. These guys are all pretty stable. Most of them are dual-diagnosed, having both substance abuse and mental problems. Symptoms should be under control by now with their meds. But the new guy, the young white one over there in the corner, he's pretty paranoid. He's been here before, a frequent flier. Dr. Larry wanted you to see what they look *before* they get stabilized."

"Fine with me."

"If things start getting out of hand, everything stops right there. We've got a couple of really good officers behind us."

Jonathon turned around and saw two huge mean in uniforms. "Hi, doc," one of them said.

Once inside the room, a couple of the men whistled as Jana took her seat. She was wearing a skirt today with a matching sweater. They men oggled her.

"Okay, knock it off, you guys. This is Mr. M, one of our new staff."

"Hi, doc."

"Hello."

"Why don't we go around the circle, starting with Lee over her on my left, and introduce ourselves? Lee?"

"Well, " Lee said shyly, "my names' Lee Johnson. I'm an alcoholic. But I ain't never hurt nobody. I keep getting arrested because I black out on the street, and then they pick me up and bring me in here."

"Thanks, Lee. Next?"

Four more men introduced themselves, told a short story of their situation in monotones, as if they had done that hundreds of times before, like a daily habit, like brushing your teeth or combing your hair. Jonathon was disappointed at the lack of spontaneity, until the 6th inmate's turn came, the new young detainee.

"The only thing that's wrong with me is that I know too much. That's why they keep bringing me back here. To drug me so that I won't talk. They say they want to help, but how can they help? They're the problem! They can't even understand. They're all Indian doctors. They're taking over the world. We white folks have to do something about it before it's too late. They're all over the place. You notice you don't see any Indian inmates? D'jou ever wonder why?"

"Alex, calm down," Jana stated, "It's true that there are several

Indian doctors here, but why do you think that's bad? They've completed medical school just like the other M.D.'s"

"Because it's a plot, what are you, stupid?"

One of the others interrupted with, "Here we go again. It's the same shit all over again with this guy. He comes back in here and ruins everything and we have to go through this paranoid crap again. I'm sick of it."

"Yeah, me too," the rest of the group mumbled. "Let's stop this bullshit right now."

"Officer!" Jana called out at that point. "Session's over!"

The door flung open and the two officers rounded everyone up and walked them out.

"Move it," they ordered.

"That could have been a potentially dangerous situation, because it could have escalated. Alex's paranoia is contagious and it does have a ring of truth to it, and he could have influenced the other inmates. Then we could have had a problem on our hands."

"Like what?" Jonathon was curious. The men didn't seem that dangerous.

"A hostage situation. I'm not kidding. A couple of years ago a white woman from the suburbs came here as a volunteer, wanting to help inmates prepare for the GED. A do-gooder. Only she didn't have any security training, and one of the first rules is, you never let yourself be isolated somewhere with an inmate. One afternoon one of her best students asked to stay behind after class to ask a few more questions. They found her unconscious in one of the bathrooms down the hall. The inmate who raped her had bragged about it to the others and one of the men turned him in."

"That's too bad, but I have to ask," Jonathon said sincerely, "why does administration post male therapists like myself on the women's unit and female therapists on the men's unit?"

"Because this place is not run according to logic and common sense. It's amazing all of us go home everyday intact. There have been some bad accidents over the years. But getting back to today, in a situation like that, always make sure you are closest to the door."

"Oh. Yeah." Jonathon mumbled. He was thinking about the volatility of the place.

"Oh, and by the way," Jana added, "You probably don't know you have a mailbox yet, but somebody else knows you have one because I checked it for you and found this letter."

"The mailboxes are on the basement level. I've got to make a couple of phone calls. See you after lunch."

Jonathon opened up the plain white envelope and read a hastily written cryptic message. It said, "When you are in the hallway through the two tunnels on your way to the cafeteria, make a sharp right turn and walk about 100 feet down the older tunnel that you'll find at that spot. I'll be there waiting for you."

"Who could this be?" Jonathon thought aloud.

"Talkin' to yourself, doc?" one of the inmates whispered behind Jonathon.

"Huh?" Jonathon said in surprise, quickly turning around. "No. I mean, yeah, I guess I was."

As he walked away, he remembered Jana's caution, "Always watch your back." He found the older tunnel off to the right and walked slowly down it for about 100 feet, then stopped. It wasn't lit very well and he could hear himself breathing. No one else seemed to be around and he was out of sight of the two main tunnels leading to the cafeteria, where there were more people around.

"Keep your voice down. Don't act startled." Some said behind him.

As Jonathon turned, he saw a tall, thin, middle aged white man in casual but neat clothes.

"Where did you come from?" he said quietly.

"Never mind that. I thought you might like to get a little run down on this place. All is not what it appears to be."

"Who are you?" Jonathon asked.

"Just someone who has worked here long enough to know a lot

and to remember every face. I'm legit, see?" The stranger flashed his I.D., but not slowly enough for Jonathon to read it.

"Point is, I know who you are and I know you're only staying a year, unlike the rest of us who seem unable to leave this place, even though we curse it every day."

"So? What's that got to do with me?"

"So, I thought that maybe when you leave, you might someday be able to help, after you germinate your experiences here."

"Help who?"

"It'll come to you."

"Why do you say that?"

"I just wanted to establish contact now. I'll tell you what. If you need some answers to those questions you most surely are going to have, just leave a plain white envelope with a black mark slashed across the top in the last mailbox on the right in the basement. It's the one that's unlabeled. If I get the envelope before noon, I'll be here when you come down for lunch. Otherwise, it'll be the next day."

"Why don't I just phone you?"

"Because the phones are bugged . Ditto for the halls and day rooms. The only places which aren't wired are the bathrooms, because that's against federal law. And down here."

Just then there was a loud bang coming from the direction leading to the cafeteria. Jonathon turned abruptly and asked, "what was that?" but when he looked back, the stranger was gone. Walking quickly back to the two tunnels, he saw nothing, and went into the cafeteria, had a quick lunch and went back to PU, women's side.

"Well, I thought you'd forgot about us," Officer Merlin laughed. "Glad you're back 'cause we got another situation to deal with here, " she said, pointing to the end of the room in the corner, where a large black woman was crouched on the floor.

"You can't force me to take no medicine, you mutha fucka's!" she screamed.

The nurse, a thin white older woman was bending over the

patient who was now on the floor, restrained by two officers, one who had his knee against the back of her neck. The nurse slipped down the back of the inmate's uniform, smoothed some alcohol on her hip, and injected her with medication.

"That'll keep her quite for a while," Merlin stated to Jonathon. "She was getting on my nerves."

"What was her problem?" Jonathon asked the nurse when she got back to the station and after the patient had been escorted to her room.

"Didn't want to take her meds."

"But, they have a right not to take them, don't they?"

"Of course they do. But if their behavior becomes disruptive and uncontrollable, we can give them a shot to calm them down, and we always do."

"Who is she?"

"Look, doc, read the chart yourself. I've got things to do," the nurse said tartly, glancing at Merlin, who was smiling wordlessly.

Jonathon pulled out the woman's chart, sat down at a desk, and began reading. The woman was in her 30's but looked older. She had a long history of mental health problems, incarceration, and institutionalizations. Homeless. Diagnosed as paranoid schizophrenic, psychotic, delusional. She was married and had 3 children. Jonathon wondered about the children. "Jesse's her name," the nurse volunteered over Jonathon's shoulder. "According to her, every male around here has made it with her. That's why we have to drag her out of the shower every morning because she fixates on washing out all the dirt that she imagines is on her. A real pain in the butt."

"Do you think part of her story might be true?" Jonathon asked.

"Lord, do you have a lot to learn!" the nurse and Officer Merlin laughed together.

"Listen, doc, when you've been around here as long as I have, you will have heard and seen it all," the nurse stated matter-of-factly. Then she got up and did an imitation of Jesse, scowling and pointing her finger in the air. "Yes sir! They did it to me! And I'm gonna get them son-of-a-bitches before they get my baby. That's all they's good for, raping!"

Merlin and the nurse were bent over in laughter. Jonathon looked up to see a bleary-eyed Jesse staring at them from the window in her room. He hoped that she didn't hear the nurse. He decided to take a break and walking outside, found Lola puffing on a cigarette.

"How's it going?" she said, exhaling.

"Oh, great, great."

"Anybody comin' on to you yet?"

"What?"

"You know what I mean! Flirting. Anyone making goo-goo eyes at you yet."

"I haven't noticed."

"Well, I have. A lot of people think you're real cute. You married?"

Jonathon was seething. Lola had gone too far. And he was in no mood to be forgiving. He has just witnessed Jessie being forcibly given a tranquilizing shot followed by the nurse doing a cruel imitation of her, in plain sight of all the other patients on the unit.

"What's that got to do with anything?" he said abruptly.

"Oh pardon me! So this place is finally getting to you. I wondered when it would."

"What do you mean?"

"You'll see. After a while, you'll get to be just like us." With that remark, she took a huge drag on her Parliament and blew the smoke out in Jonathon's face before walking away to play pool.

Jonathon turned and pulled a white envelope out of his pocket, slashed a black line across the top with a marking pen, found the mailbox area, and place it in the last mailbox. Then he decided that he would go home early.

The next morning, Jonathon felt no enthusiasm when he opened the door to the PU. Jesse was up and about. She looked much better than last night. She even smiled shyly when she saw him. He pulled out her chart and motioned her to follow him into one of the interview rooms.

"Hello, Jessie. I'm Dr. M."

"Oh, hi! I've heard all about you," Jessie said with a big toothless grin on her face.

"That's good! But I wanted to ask you about yesterday."

"Jessie's demeanor changed dramatically. Her face darkened and she scowled.

"Those bitches," she muttered.

"Who?"

"That guard and the nurse. They've always got it in for me. I know them. Every night one of them lets the male guards in from over on the other side so that he can rape me. I keep telling them about it, but they just laugh and stick me with needles."

"Do you know who did it?" Jonathon asked, looking earnest.

"It's a whole bunch of them. They take turns."

Jonathon took a deep breath, thinking, "she *is* delusional." Then he began to go through the standard questions.

"Do you feel like harming yourself or others? Are you hearing voices?"

Jessie looked at him with no expression on her face, got up slowly and walked right out of the room.

"Hey! Where do you think you're going! Doc ain't finished with you yet!" Merlin shouted.

"No, no. It's okay, Officer. She can go back."

"Well, all right then."

Jessie shot one last look of disgust at Jonathon before she went into her room. Jonathon felt oddly uncomfortable. He picked up his notebook and pen and went to have a cup of coffee. On the way to the cafeteria, he passed the dark tunnel on the right, paused, and then decided to see if his strange friend would be there.

"Over here," the voice said.

"I'm glad to see you, whoever you are," Jonathon said with relief.

"What happened?"

Jonathon told Mr. X what had happened yesterday and his disappointing interview with Jessie today.

"Why should that bother you?"

"Because it seems that she was given a shot only because she refused her medication, which is her legal right. It seems to me that she was being punished for exercising her legal rights."

"So?"

"How can you think that way?"

"I don't necessarily think that way," X responded, "but when you've been here as long as I have you will begin to see that's how things are run around here. Rules don't matter. Do you think if crazy Jessie gets out of here, she's going to tell anybody who can do something about it, about what may or may not have happened to her? And let's suppose that she did find someone to believe her, and that person filed a complaint on her behalf. What good do you think that would do?"

Jonathon stared straight ahead.

"Besides," X added, "she *has* been raped by officers."

"What!" Jonathon shouted.

"Keep it down, I told you! I can't be seen talking to you."

"How could such a thing happen?"

"Easy. It's night-time. The officers on duty are asleep. Another officer comes on the unit to run interference. Another one goes into Jessie's room. She's half delirious anyway and probably doesn't realize what's happening to her."

"But how can the officers do such a thing?"

"Look. There's some very decent officers here. There are also some real problems. You can't work in a place like this without having it affect you negatively."

"What about you? You seem pretty normal to me," Jonathon said pointedly.

"I work at it. I have a life on the outside. A lot of people who work here don't. They're very sick. What kind of person could enjoy this kind of job, keeping people caged up? Enslaving others? It's much easier to think of them, the inmates, as sub-human.

Then you can do anything to them, because they're not like you at all."

"I find that disgusting."

"Of course you do. I do, too. But you'll hear about inmate-officer sex, officer-officer sex, and all gender sex."

"When and where does all this go on?"

"All the time. No, I stand corrected. More in the evenings and on weekends, when the supervisors are tired and sloppy. There's one notorious unit on the second floor that hasn't been opened since the building opened and probably never will be opened for patients, because it is now used for another purpose."

"You mean?"

"Yeah, it's the hottest thing some people got going here."

"You make it sound like some kind of playboy club, instead of a jail, complete with liquor and drugs."

"That's just it. It is."

"How can this be?"

"It's really true about you, what they say, isn't it?

"What, that I'm naive? I don't care. I happen to believe that our system has values."

"Pardon me. But you'll have to adjust your vision now, won't you?"

"Look, whoever you are. I do know something about what goes on in jails. For instance, I know that inmates make a crude form of alcohol, that they sometimes get dope in here."

"Hooch. It's called hooch. They let the fruit ferment."

"Okay, hooch. So I would assume that if that's allowed, anything goes."

"Well," X continued, "they can't really stop it. They do searches every now and then. We have lock-downs. But human behavior returns to what it has always been. You can't keep a man captive forever. It's awfully hard to crush the human spirit of rebellion. You can't change the way an incarcerated population behaves and how they are going to find their outlets."

"All right, all right. But how do the drugs get in?"

"That's the easy part. Think about it. They don't walk in on the rats and cockroaches."

"Visitors?"

"Sometimes. But more often it's the officers, most of whom belong to gangs themselves. They're real good at bringing it in. It's a great second income."

"Why do people around here, I mean the ones in control, " Jonathon mused," act so tough when they are just as bad as the inmates?"

"You just answered your own question. They act tough because they can't do anything and they don't want to do anything. They're all in this together. And those kinds of people are dangerous, because they're sick individuals. They are living a lie."

"I've got to get back," Jonathon said, turning. "Don't leave yet. When can I see you again?" But X was already gone, disappeared silently down one of the dark mazes which ran under the cells.

As the weeks flew by, Jonathon began to see a kind of rhythm to the admissions to the PU. Most of the patient-inmates were primarily substance-abusers with mental illnesses or mentally ill with substance abuse problems secondarily. Very few of them were violent or abusive toward the staff. Few of them refused their psychiatric medications. Most of the time the medications did help them. After a few days they were cleaner, sober, and almost normal when spoken to. Only when one attempted a deep conversation did their pathology come out.

Many of the staff, including the officers, were decent people who tried to help the inmates. Very few in fact were sadistic, but those that were, stood out and gave the staff a bad name. Jonathon never personally saw any sexual abuse by an officer toward an inmate. But the stories went around every once in a while.

He met dozens of people whose livelihoods depended upon the incarceration of others. But few people who could really help. One of them was a social worker with whom Jonathon often had lunch.

"I've been hearing all these stories about you," Jeff said the first time they met. "Like how you really take patients seriously and listen to their stories like it's gospel and other naive stuff."

"Anything wrong with taking a patient seriously?" Jonathon replied.

"Oh, absolutely not, don't take me wrong. It warms my heart."

Jonathon became inured, as everyone said he would, to the jaded atmosphere, eventually. He found himself liking Jeff despite his sarcasm.

"I'm glad we met," he added. "Many of the women on PU ask to see a social worker and I wondered if there even were any around. Some of the patients want to call home and they can't seem to do it on the pay phones."

"That's because 95% of their families have blocks on their phones. Any why is that? Because they are sick and tired of getting collect calls from these black sheep who continue to screw up their lives, who continue to get arrested, who won't stop drinking or taking drugs, who won't get a job, and who dump their illegitimate offspring on them, and ask for money besides. Wouldn't you put a block on your phone too?"

"I know what you're saying is true a lot of the time, but some of them have valid issues. They have welfare checks in their mailboxes which could be used to bail them out."

"To go where?" Jeff challenged.

"Well, to . . ." Jonathon started to answer, but then realized he didn't know what to say.

"Look, pal, stay cool and I'll catch you later, okay? And stop taking everything so seriously."

The next day, Jonathon took a right turn at the middle of the tunnel. He walked about 100 feet, stopped and waited. There was not sound for 5 minutes and just when he was about to go back he heard X's voice, "What now?"

"I'm glad you're here! I didn't think you got my message."

"I always get them, don't worry about that. What's up?"

"Well, I was wondering about something."

"Uh-huh."

"I found a list of shelters and rehab centers that the social worker Jeff had left behind on the desk in PU one night. I thought it was great. It had over 150 shelters listed for the homeless and over 80 free drug counseling organizations on it. I made copies and handed them out to the patients yesterday. Dr. Larry walked by while I was doing that and he practically swore me off the unit."

"And you don't know why."

"Well. Yeah."

"Do you know anything about that list?" X asked blandly.

"You mean who made it?"

"No. The places on it."

"No."

"Do you always jump across a chasm before you know its distance?"

"Okay, okay."

"Have you ever seen a homeless shelter?"

"No."

"You should. They are crammed full. They have a 3 month long waiting list for new residents. Those that get in are lucky."

"You mean they have no room for the patients I have been sending there."

"You got it."

"So what I have been doing is useless. Cruel, too. Giving these women hope when there isn't any."

"Sorry."

"Well, what's the point of even having a list? What good is a social worker in a place like this?"

X looked sadly at Jonathon and said. "You're missing the big question."

"You mean, where they go, when they can't get into a shelter."

"Right. Back into the streets and alleys where they came from. They try to stay off drugs for a while. They try to stay on their meds. But sooner or later someone comes along and offers them some free bliss. And they're hooked again. Then they have to support their habit, so they start stealing or prostituting, not for food, but for drugs."

"It's disgusting and pathetic."

"Yes it is."

"Can't anyone do anything? What about the judges?"

"You're dreaming again. Most of these inmates, when they go to court, they get up at 5 A.M. They sit on a bench for 6 hours. They go in front of a judge who doesn't even look at them. They meet their court-appointed lawyer for the first time that day, and he or she hasn't even read their case. The judge and attorney say a couple of words to each other in legal jargon, and it's all over before the inmate even knows it's begun. And so on."

"What about the cases in the papers and on TV?"

"The exceptions to the rule, because they are high-profile. Like the inmate who put her baby in a microwave. Or the mother who cut up her 2 year old because he was beaten to death by her boyfriend and she had to destroy the evidence. Or the grandmother who hanged her grandchild. Those are high profile cases and the pro bono attorneys don't mind taking them because they get a lot of publicity which brings in paying clients. The stories are so gross and shocking, that's why they're in the news, because people like to hear about horror, about deviance, about how evil-evil can really be. But the great masses of miserable ordinary people inside these walls, no one hears or cares about."

"I think I'm going to go now," Jonathon said, experiencing a sinking feeling in his gut.

"I know. I'm always here when you need me."

Jonathon was coming to the third quarter of his fellowship. He decided to have a long talk with Dr. Larry.

"I guess what I want to say is that it's more discouraging around here than I ever expected," he confessed.

"It happens!" Dr. Larry cheerfully acknowledged.

"I'm serious, Dr. Larry. I don't understand what happened to the ideal of helping others. Psychiatry, the profession that I had hoped to go into, is about that-helping others. Making them well again. I find very little of that going on here."

"Did you say that you *had hoped* to go into? You mean you've changed your mind?"

"No. I'm only saying."

"What you're doing is what every Do-Gooder does when he comes here, from the research scientist to the religious fanatic. They think they have all the answers. They all believe that their brand of therapy will change these people. You don't understand, it's not about therapy. It's not about helping anyone. It's about keeping them housed, fed and quiet until they get out of here."

"But . . ."

"Eventually those bright eyes of yours will glaze over, like the rest of ours' did, and when you hear for the hundredth time about how a patient was abused as a child and how he or she has had such a rotten life, that that's why he or she takes drugs, because it's so hard out there, because they had to give up their child to foster care, etc. etc. Then, at last you will develop your own style. It will be more balanced than what you do now. You will be harder on them and easier on yourself. You will force them to take responsibility for the life that God gave them, instead of squandering it away."

"That's fair, Dr. Larry. But some things I have seen and heard about constitute patient abuse."

"Like what." Dr. Larry was irritated.

"Like Jessie, who claims she was raped by officers. No one investigated. They just assumed she was crazy. Like Mary, who is sent to a shelter which will never be able to take her because they have no room. Like Josie, who isn't allowed to attend her son's funeral."

"You know what, Mr. M.?"

"Dr. Miracle."

"Oh, pardon, me, it's Dr. Miracle now. You know what, Dr. Miracle, you'd better keep your mouth shut about the things you hear and see around here. I'm not the one to fear, but if word gets around, I wouldn't want to see you hurt."

"Are you threatening me?"

"Don't take yourself so seriously."

Jonathon could hardly believe what had just transpired. Larry walked away briskly.

"One on the new!" Merlin announced with gusto.

Jonathon pulled out some forms and his pen and turn to face the new inmate, Vicki, who bent over at the waist and through up all over his desk.

"Bitch! Slob! Get over here and sit down. Now!" The two officers who had brought her in shouted. Jonathon picked up a few paper towels.

"Don't you dare to that!" the nurse lurched forward and pulled Jonathon back.

"Are you crazy? She's HIV positive, she has hepatitis C and TB. A total loss. I'm calling the Environmental Department to clean this up. Don't touch anything. Here, put some gloves and a mask on."

Jonathon stepped back and observed Vicki, who had heard everything the nurse had said. She did indeed look ill, but not as ill as one would think, knowing that she was so diseased. What was most striking about her was the fact that she was 9 month's pregnant.

After Vicki was cleaned up, strip-searched, and given a beige maternity uniform, she was brought into the interview room where Jonathon was waiting for her.

"Do I know you? You new here/" she said in a child-like voice.

Jonathon glanced at her record. It listed her hear of birth as 1970. Vicki was only 20 years old, a heroin addict, mother of 3, HIV positive and a hepatitis carrier. The TB could be treated.

"How do you feel?" ventured Jonathon, looking up.

"What's your name? Don't I even get to know your name?" she said plaintively.

"I'm Mr. M . . .I'm Dr. Miracle," Jonathon replied.

"Miracle? Is that your name?"

"Yes, I'm afraid so."

"Well, I really deserve a miracle, you know. My baby's due any minute and look where I am now."

"Why were sent to this unit?"

"Because those cops got it in for me. They just see me walkin' down the street and they pick me up and say anything they want about me and nobody believes me."

"What's your charge?"

"Soliciting and possession. How could I be soliciting like I am?"

"But you do have a history of drug use."

"But I'm clean now, and I'm not crazy I don't want to hurt my baby. I stopped the heroin months ago, and they slipped cocaine on me."

"Okay, okay, don't be upset. At least you're in a clean place where you can take a shower and sleep in a bed. I'm sure you'll be moved to the medical unit or to the hospital in a few hours. I will stop in and see you in a short while."

Jonathon got some coffee, passing Lola puffing on her ubiquitous Parliament.

"I hear you got a frequent flier up there."

"Vicki?"

"She looks like she's ready to drop that baby any minute, don't she?"

"Yeah, she does."

The coffee tasted so good that Jonathon had several cups of it. He wasn't in any hurry to get back, but he had several hours to go. He reluctantly stood up and walked down the tunnel and paused before the hall which veered off to the right. He hadn't seen X in a while and he really needed to talk to him. He walked down the tunnel.

"I know what you must be thinking," X whispered.

"Oh! I didn't think you'd be here."

"When I heard that you got Vicki up there, I figured you'd be impressed."

"Yeah, but not favorably."

"She's quite a fighter. Her mother's boyfriend raped her when she was 6. Then her mother died in front of her when she was 12. She started using when she was 14, when she got pregnant for the first time. A well-know prostitute drug addict."

"It's really depressing."

"Of course it is. But you're supposed to be professional. You're supposed to be able to take it."

"Doesn't it ever get to you?"

"Of course it does. But I've been here for a while. Most people forget the humanity. I still see it, but there's nothing I can do to help. Vicki, when she isn't a street person, lives with a pimp. The two children she had when she was younger are living with foster parents, and that's probably a good thing. On other occasions when she's been here, I've sat down on the floor with her and tried to talk some sense into her. But it's hard. What chances does a poor young black woman with a 7th grade education have in this world? It's tough."

"I'm not saying I support abortion, but isn't there some way to keep her from bringing more children into this world, who are going to live a miserable existence, be born with HIV and addicted to heroin or cocaine?"

"No. Unfortunately, there isn't anything anyone can do. If the judge doesn't mandate her to an institution, after she serves a little time, she'll be out on the streets again. She'll take her medicine for a little while, then stop, and begin the whole cycle again."

"Well, can't she be convinced to be sterilized, given her history?"

"That's social engineering and as liberal as I am, I've thought of it too, but there would be a loud cry out there about patient rights if that were to happen."

"Then it seems that the only way someone like Vicki can be helped is for her to want to change. Can't someone be assigned to her on a daily basis and perhaps convince her to live differently and give her some good reasons to try?"

"You still haven't gotten it. *They don't care. Nobody here cares.* Remember that. I have to go now."

Jonathon leaned against the wall in that dark, musty, mildewy tunnel for a long while after X left. He was a good man, smart, hadn't let the system wear him down completely, but there wasn't much he could do.

With a heavy heart, Jonathon walked back up the steps to PU, where as he opened the door, he was met with loud screams, telephones ringing, and the sound of people running across the room. Several female officers pushed past Jonathon. There were two nurses in Vicki's room and the physician was being paged continuously. "She's in labor," Jonathon thought, and sat down.

Feeling useless, Jonathon sat down at the desk and answered the phone. Dr. Larry called. Lola called. Jana called. Even X called. "I heard. How are you holding up?" he joked. It must have been a quick labor because within a few minutes, Jonathon heard, "here she comes" from the nurses. The screams of discomfort subsided. The scene had transformed into one of joy. Jonathon couldn't restrain himself. He left the desk and walked over to Vicki's room. The doctor was holding a tiny baby boy who seemed lifeless until he slowly yawned. Vicki was trying desperately to turn on her side to see him, but her wrists were handcuffed to the bed. She looked up at Jonathon and smiled weakly. "There's my miracle," she said.

Jonathon walked away, his mind churning. Officer Merlin came up beside him and asked him if he had ever seen a birth before. "No, I don't think I have. I don't mean the birth, I mean this kind of birth, where the mother is chained to a bed!"

"Oh no, here we go again," Merlin quipped. "I think it's time we parted ways for a while."

Jonathon thought, "yeah, me too", although he personally like Officer Merlin, but he was experiencing sensory overload. The nurses whisked past him rolling an incubator with the new baby in it.

"Are they both going to maternity?" he asked.

"What are you nuts? Of course not. Don't you know what happens when you have a baby in jail?"

"No, how would I?"

"The baby is taken immediately out of the room after being born. The mother doesn't even get to see it, let alone hold it."

"I believe it. And the baby goes where?"

"To the hospital, then if it survives, out to foster care. This baby has a lot of problems. Probably no one will want to adopt him, given his mother's HIV and drug addiction." Everyone laughed as if it were a joke. Merriment filled the unit.

Jonathon sat back in his chair, picked up the phone and called his advisor at his medical school. "I have a message for you. Please don't respond after I tell you. Let me hang up. I'm dropping out of medical school."

A year later his wife had divorced him and Jonathon had entered law school.

CHAPTER THREE

The Holy City

The dream always ended the same way. The gloom which always followed on the heels of the rage and helplessness he felt upon awakening was starting to settle in. Since those days at Block County Jail, Jonathon had rekindled in his mind the idea that jails and prisons were better places for some people than the streets and alleys they had come from. He knew that some divorces, like his own, were meant to be. His incarcerated brother was eventually granted clemency because of Jonathon's efforts while in law school. He had come a long way from Block County Jail.

At the moment, however, he faced a new experience: Jerusalem, as the plane touched down at Tel Aviv Airport. Having heard claims to the "the Holy City' by both Arabs and Israelis, and having no opinion about the matter himself, Jonathon approached this historic relic of a metropolis somewhat deftly, so as to avoid being subdued by its spell before he could perceive it in his own way. Yet once there, he set about his main task immediately, devising the initial version of the appellate statement on a laptop in his hotel.

Afterwards, drained physically, intellectually, and emotionally, he went for a long, solitary walk, his chosen activity when he needed to get back to himself, away from people, from their projections on him. He yearned at those times, to become anonymous in the crowd, completely unreachable by phone, fax or e-mail. He entered the ancient city of Jerusalem via the Jaffa Gate and walked for what seemed to be miles amidst labyrinthian alleys lined with shops.

The marketplace was teeming, yet he had no desire to by anything. For whom? There was no wife, lover, child in his life.

But of course he had chosen to relinquish those accouterments of normal living and was reconciled to his decision. Work was his only mission now. Today his main purpose was to absorb a sense of the soul of the people who had inhabited this land for thousands of years. Walking along aimlessly down one street and up another, he found himself suddenly at the entrance to the magnificent Al-Aqsa Mosque, then the next moment before the Wailing Wall. The overlap of cultures and beliefs was in a way, mesmerizing. But in an equal sense it could be quite destabilizing.

The peculiar juxtaposition-the sight of praying Moslems and Jews, within a few feet of each other, created an eerie sense of dissociation within himself, a loss of bearings, an existential angst. Jonathon, perhaps because of jet-lag, did not find this apprehension disagreeable. In fact, it was stimulating. It brought with it memories of his childhood. He thought of himself and his brother as children, habituating to their milieu naturally, without questioning fate, unconsciously almost, becoming much like those around them. No one realized at the time of childhood what was happening, that they were being shaped and molded, because it occurred so innocuously in every culture.

There are not lessons in how to become an American, an Iranian, an Israeli, and Egyptian, or a Palestinian. The formation of an identity occurs during the process of interaction between the inner self and the socially-responding self, almost, but not quite, unconsciously. One day, each of us realizes that we are carbon copies of everyone else and can be differentiated from the masses only with great effort. Our hubris of individuality is nothing more than self-deception.

Caught in this reverie, Jonathon glanced up and with a start, found himself at a signpost which read, "Via Dolorosa". Absolutely, he thought, I must go on. He walked unevenly up a steep, narrow street where Christ supposedly carried his cross, was crowned with thorns, spat upon, and flogged. The street also led to the place of his crucifixion, the "King of the Jews", his burial place marked by an ornate and ancient Christian monument, the Church of the Holy Sepulcher.

Tracing his way back through the maze by which he had come, Jonathon felt invigorated. As a child he had absorbed the traditional teachings of Christ somewhat mindlessly, but now, seeing the streets where he walked and preached, he had a radically different perspective. The public man, the humble sufferer was nonetheless a brilliant anarchist, Jonathon thought, never desiring to become an idol of worship for fanatics.

Suddenly, the whole situation seemed incredibly funny and Jonathon needed a good, strong cup of coffee. In an obscure corner before him was a quiet coffee house. He sank his tired body into the folds of a huge leather chair and sipped on a double cappuccino while reading the *Jerusalem Post*. Hours later, it seemed, he found his way back to the hotel which the CIA had arranged for him, the American Colony.

After falling into a fitful sleep, Jonathon dreamt that he was walking along the route in East Jerusalem which he had taken earlier in the day. This time the shops were closed and no one was around. The ambience was entirely different without the human element, sort of like walking into a de Chirico surrealist painting. Looking up, he noticed a large Grecian urn perched precariously at the corner of a balustrade. The urn began to sway almost imperceptibly at first, then violently, until it became apparent that it was going to fall at any moment. Jonathon stood motionless in the path of the fall, unable to move, as the urn cascaded toward him. Only with great effort and at the last possible moment was he able to drag his reluctant body to the side of the street, as two things occurred simultaneously, one unconsciously-the vase crashed into a thousand pieces at his feet, and the other, consciously-the hotel phone rang loudly and rudely about an inch from his ear.

"Yes," he responded immediately.

"Jonathon! It's PSYCOPS. Good morning! Are you all right?"

"Just fine, thanks. What's up?" Jonathon replied flatly, still thinking about the shattered Grecian urn at his feet in the dream.

"Slight adjustment. Dr. McIntyre can't be with you today as your expert witness. He's in Africa involved in some sort of investigation of a strange bacterial outbreak."

"Listen, I was relying on him. I needed him to describe the role of neurotransmitters, depression, and the alterations on both which are effected by LSD. What am I supposed to do now?" Jonathon bemoaned.

"Don't panic! He, McIntyre that is, sends his greetings and apologies. Apparently he was a professor of yours at some time?"

"Yeah, that's right. Once upon a time I was in medical school."

"Well, that may be why he said you would have no problem understanding the documents he faxed to me today to give to you."

Jonathon smiled, thinking of his old eccentric professor, one of the most brilliant in medical school. "What do you make of the documents, PSYCOPS?"

"Well, they look like Greek to me, to tell you the truth. I just dropped them off at your hotel about an hour ago."

"Okay. I'll have a look at them and see you in court, then?" Jonathon ventured.

"Absolutely! We've sent over a taxi for you. The driver's name is Omar."

"Thanks. See you later," Jonathon mumbled as he glanced at his watch. It was 6 A.M. The appeal was scheduled at 10 A.M. "Damned anal-retentives," he said as he turned over to sleep one last hour.

"Good morning, Ya Syed! Omar at your service! How are you this morning?" Omar, the congenial taxi driver provided by PSYCOPS, displayed a wide grin of crooked teeth stained by cigarettes and coffee, as he gestured into his aging vehicle decorated with small Palestinian flags.

"Good morning. Is it Omar? I'm fine, thank you. Can you

take me to the Palestinian-Israeli Joint Government Building? I
believe it's at . . . . " Jonathon shuffled through his papers.

"Not to worry, Ya Syed, Omar knows where you want to go.
Please, please get in. We will be there very soon. Relax! You are
going to win the young American's trial today, God willing," Omar,
the consummate wiry Arab entrepreneur, who, from his taxi, cold
procure almost anything one's heart might desire from German
Deutschmark to Russian caviar, was being particularly bunt this
morning. With this passenger, he felt it was the best way.

"How did you know I was his attorney?" Jonathon replied
suspiciously, already annoyed at PSYCOPS taking over his life in
the Middle East.

"But I didn't know! You just told me," Omar laughed
uproariously. "Don't worry. Allah is on your side, and so is Omar.
How could you possibly lose?" More raucous laughter. "Music?
How about a cigarette?"

Before Jonathon could answer, the undulating tones of a solo
flute with drum accompaniment seeped through the car's ancient
speakers, followed shortly by a female voice which seemed to by
lyrically describing the most exquisite torture. Resigned to being
Omar's captive, Jonathon took a deep breath, decline the proffered
Gitanne cigarette, and leafed through the morning edition of *The
Jerusalem Post*. The ride wore on and on. Jonathon glanced at his watch.

"Omar! Where ARE we!" he shouted over the music.

"We are in the shopping area of Jabel Mukaber. Much foreign
money built it. Interesting, is it not? I thought you might like to
see it," Omar responded, cordially.

"What! Omar, I need to be at the Courthouse as soon as
possible. You must know that already. I'm not particularly interested
in sight-seeing today."

"Very good. Very good. I am taking you a good way, you will
see. Do you want to see all of the photographers and news people
who are waiting for you?" Omar asked sheepishly.

"No! Absolutely not! Of course not, they are the last people I
want to see."

"The you must trust Omar, Ya Syed. Omar will get you there. No photographs. No nothing."

"Thank you," Jonathon replied, feeling somewhat helpless at the realization that he was completely in the hands of this strange creature, a Palestinian taxi driver in Jerusalem. Finally they arrived at the back entrance of the Courthouse. Omar opened the door of the car and motioned for Jonathon to disembark. A door to the building suddenly opened, as if on cue, which is the way everything else seemed to be happening since he arrived, Jonathon thought.

"Ahlain wa Sallan. Ahlain. Ahlain. Ahlain." These greetings were repeated several times as an apparent court clerk opened the back door for Omar and Jonathon. They were expecting him, Jonathon thought, but he was not uncomfortable about it. The man who opened the door was dressed in jeans, a t-shirt, and the black and white Palestinian kaffiyeh, made famous by Yasser Arafat, where it was always perched atop his head.

"Omar, why are we using the back door, by the way?" Jonathon ventured.

"Malish, Mr. Jonathon, malish. You will understand."

It occurred to Jonathon that, while not formally introducing himself to Omar, he seemed to know everything about him. There was no time for further musings as Omar, Jonathon, and the third man—-Jonathon didn't know what to think of that person-was he a servant, janitor, or CIA operative?-walked briskly down a long, dark hallway to a small ante room with smoky windows overlooking the street at the front of the building. Jonathon peered our of the dim windows. He was, at that moment, eternally grateful to Omar for providing an alternative entrance to the Courthouse other than the obvious front one.

For there, an unusual assembly was gathering composed of journalists, housewives, children, businessmen, Imams, Rabbis, students, and teachers. Their discourse was discernable and constant, punctuated by intermittent outbursts. "I am sick to death of all this coddling of drug addicts!" one woman shouted. "Why should the government spend our taxes rehabilitating them? They broke

the law. Let them pay for it in prison where they belong!" Rousing
cheers followed.

Then, from a dissenter, "Have we become a society without
compassion? Just because someone has made a mistake doesn't mean
they must forfeit their lives forever. They can work in the community
for their sentences. There is plenty of work around here that nobody
seems willing to do."

The centrists chimed in. "Life is worth more than money! When
they get out of prison, they've learned to be real criminals by then.
They should spend some of their time in prison, but not all of it,
then work in the community, provided they are non-violent."

Small discussions were taking place among the groups. One
common ground was the attack on academics. "What is your
solution anyway, with your big ideas from the university! Get out
of your ivory tower and live in the real world, where every dollar
counts."

Tremendous applause from all sides. The university group,
oblivious to the undisguised criticism, continued to pass out papers
inviting everyone to a lecture on the subject. Jonathon sighed. It
was the same confrontation all over again, about what to do with
drug offenders: imprison them, treat them, banish them, kill them?
There were feisty thundering moralistic platitudes from the right,
compassionate liberal assertions from the left, unworkable and
complex feasibility plans from the academics, and the journalists,
who just wanted a piece of the action. It could have been L.A.,
New York, San Francisco, or Chicago.

"Is Mr. Jonathon angry with Omar?" the taxi driver looked
remorseful.

"Of course not, Omar. What you did makes perfect sense now.
You were protecting me from all those people and photographers.
Thank you, by all means."

"This is true, Ya Syed. But, malish, never mind. What about
some coffee? A cigarette?"

Before Jonathon could respond, the door to the room opened
suddenly and in stepped PSYCOPS. "Well, good morning, Jonathon!

Everything okay? Did Omar take good care of you? Good. Good. We are ready and presume that you are. Of course, you must have noticed the crowed gathering outside. Unfortunately, the Michael Bateson drug case has generated a lot of publicity-exactly what you were hoping to avoid-but we're counting on you to go smoothly and quickly, right, Jonathon? Time to go! Good luck." PSYCOPS disappeared as quickly as he had appeared a moment ago.

"Good luck, too, Mr. Jonathon. Insha'allah!" Omar added.

"Thank you. If you don't mind, I would like a few moments alone to coordinate my thoughts. I need at least 10 minutes, PSYCOPS."

In medical school, many years ago, Jonathon had learned a technique of intense concentration called the "flow state." Confirmed with PET scans, the flow state evolved during a time of peak performance, during which a burst of alpha waves occurred in the left side of the brain. That area was more identified with language and analytical skills. During the flow state, it was this side which relaxed, allowing the right side of the brain, more identified with spatial relations and pattern recognition, to dominate, temporarily. The experiment suggested that it was possible to produce this phenomenon of increasing alpha waves consciously, with training, very similar to biofeedback. It was a matter of practicing a self-devised routine relevant to the activity just before beginning it. By this method one entered the zone of concentration, where attention becomes heightened to relevant cues about the particular subject. In the zone, internal talk and other distractions were minimal. The advantage to experiencing and maintaining the flow state before an important event such as the presentation of a legal argument, was that one's concentration would be razor-sharp.

Jonathon's personal routine was to slowly arrange his notes and pens as the first step. This manual tidying up prepared him to be receptive to the imagery he would focus on while mentally rehearsing his legal strategy.

Dr. McIntyre, his former medical school professor and mentor, called it "fine-tuning the neural circuits". It worked. As an excellent adjunct to the exercise, Jonathon repeated positive self-talk, a personal running commentary about his strengths. This left no room whatsoever for negativity of any kind to slip through to waste energy. That was to be avoided at all costs at these moments because mental acuity can be easily sidetracked to engage in useless ruminations, instead of more finely tuning neural circuits. Jonathon thought of it as a form of mental athletics. He closed his eyes, focusing on the task at hand, obliterating all else, and imagined himself going through his paces as one of the top criminal defense attorneys in the world. He envisioned a stunning victory. He re-enacted his grandest moment, when he was able, through sheer rhetoric and logic, to convince 13 judges to overturn his brother's 20 year sentence for a nonviolent drug offense.

That was a classic trial. The evil enemy was the disgruntled prosecutor and the judge was a captive audience. It was not only a battle of facts against innuendo, but a struggle for the winning interpretation of those facts. Much rested on the attorney's complete belief that his client was innocent. The prosecutors did not have strength of conviction behind their opinions. Somewhere in their minds, they thought, 'thank god this is not my brother'. Somewhere in their unconscious a private battle was going on between the law they were sworn to uphold, as it was interpreted to them, and their private morality.

To favor the external interpretation over their deeply personal sense of fairness and morality forces a person to exist on a plane of ambiguity and self-deception. That is not a very healthy way to live. Jonathon, however, was clear about his priorities. They were in order. He was ready.

Courtroom the world over look alike: dark mahogany, oppressive silence. Jonathon fought back a slight feeling of nausea he always felt when he walked into a courtroom. Had he forgotten his notes? Was it the wrong day, the wrong hour? The onset of last-minute anxieties was as predictable as his ritual of mental preparation. It always ended a few minutes before he would speak. He hoped that this would happen now also. He would make a definite choice of which force he would allow to dominate, fear or confidence.

Confidence was winning so far. The alpha waves began to have their effect. Now he relished his role as the center of everyone's attention for this short but crucial time. Today, flanked by PSYCOPS and two secret service men who appeared out of nowhere, Jonathon would be a champion for the truth.

He knew that every eye was focused on him as he walked to his place at the defendant's table. There was a great deal of incoherent mumbling going on. Was it supportive of him of disapproving? Since a convicted prisoner on appeal need not be present, Jonathon embodied not only the identity of the defendant's counsel, but that of the accused as well.

Three appellate judges strode in with great ceremony: two Palestinians and one Israeli. The Palestinians wore poker-straight self-conscious expressions on their faces while the Israeli, watching everything carefully, exhibited what appeared to be a sly grin. Was that a concealed penchant for humor or the sadism which comes with power, Jonathon wondered. Then, chiding himself, he thought, "No time for idle thoughts."

His presentation was about to begin. Jonathon Miracle arose and spoke in a confident measured voice. "Your Honors, my client Michael Bateson, the Petitioner, has set forth claims in this court establishing that he is entitled to relief under Section 2255."

"Your Honors, as counsel for the Petitioner, I appear in support of his motion to vacate or to set aside his sentence, handed down by the lower court in Jerusalem exactly three months ago: on one count of conspiracy to possess with intent to distribute LSD, in violation of 21 P.I.C. § 841 (a) and § 846 and 18 P.I.C. § 2, and one count of conspiracy to possess with intent to distribute psilocybin in violation of the same statues. The Petitioner pleased not guilty, was tried by jury, testified at his trial, and requests an appeal of his conviction."

"On September 14, Petitioner left his home in East Jerusalem to participate in a "Swap Meet", a sort of open-air bazaar which has been held in the neutral trading zone between East Jerusalem in Palestine and West Jerusalem in Israel every Sunday for several years. At this market, merchants sell arts and crafts, paintings, clothes, food, and many other items to passers-by, who are comprised mostly of tourists. Petitioner has been supporting himself by selling embroidered jackets which he imports from Guatemala, at the Swap-Meet for about one year. He is no newcomer to the scene. The local people all know and like him. Since it is to the advantage of a merchant to be at these Swap-Meets early, Petitioner arrived at 8:00 A.M. to set up his booth. At about 11:00 A.M. he was joined by Wally Wausau, a friend, who had been visiting the Petitioner at his home the night before. Petitioner had not seen Mr. Wausau for four years. They knew each other from concerts they had attended in the United States.

At that point, Petitioner left Mr. Wausau in charge of his wares while he went to get lunch. Upon his return, he found a disturbance had developed. His friend Mr. Wausau was involved in hand to hand fighting with several policemen. Petitioner attempted to intervene and was subdued and taken into custody along with Mr. Wausau. Both men were charged with possession with intent to sell LSD and psilocybin, as outlined in the record. Petitioner subsequently pleased not guilty while Mr. Wausau pleaded to all charged on a plea-bargaining agreement arranged by the prosecutor. Petitioner was originally scheduled to be tried with his co-defendant. But by Mr. Wausau already being sentenced to a term of 188 months in an Israeli prison, my client was to be tried alone.

"At his trial, Petitioner pleaded that he was unaware that Mr. Wausau had in his possession a large quantity of LSD and psilocybin mushroom, or that he had been attempting to sell these illicit drugs to passers-by at the Swap-Meet. On cross-examination by the government, Petitioner was asked if he had been involved in an incident the preceding year in Florida, when the American State Police had stopped the van he was driving and found a controlled substance in a knapsack.

"Despite Petitioner's objections that the questions violated

P.I.R. Evid 404 (b), the Court rules that the government could continue it questioning in order to show Petitioner's motive in the present case. Petitioner refused to testify, invoking his right against self-incrimination. At the close of the trial, the Judge instructed the jury, inter alia, it could draw inferences from the Petitioner's refusal to testify while being cross-examined.

"One of the witnesses for the prosecution, a woman who had been within a few feet from Mr. Wausau testified that she heard him ask a man with whom he had struck up a conversation, if he would be interested in buying contraband drugs. She also stated that the Petitioner was present when this occurred. It was this witness who summoned the police, who were in fact nearby. They searched Mr. Wausau's rather large camping bag, finding LSD and mushrooms. Both Mr. Wausau and Petitioner were immediately arrested. Mr. Wausau was sentenced to 181 months, a more lenient sentence than the sentencing guidelines would recommend, because he admitted his guilt, while the Petitioner was given a sentence of 235 months. This sentence was calculated using mandatory minimum sentencing guidelines and by adding a two-level enhancement for the obstruction of justice which supposedly occurred because although he had pleaded innocent, he was in fact found guilty by the jury. His claim of innocence was thus interpreted as an obstruction to justice and refusal to incriminate himself as an indication of duplicity.

"Counsel would like to bring to the Court's attention the following points:

1. When the prosecution introduced the charge that the Petitioner had been arrested the previous year when drugs were found in his van, his court-appointed attorney at the time objected to that inclusion, since Petitioner had not been tried nor convicted on that charge or on any other charge up to that time. As a matter of fact, he had no criminal record whatsoever. The Court improperly permitted the government to question Petitioner about a prior "bad act" in violent of P.I.R. Evid. 404 (b). Evidence of prior "bad acts" is only admissible by the court if it is similar enough to the

present crime to be relevant and if the value of the evidence is not outweighed by the danger of unfair prejudice."Petitioner has compelling grounds for appeal on a number of points. The statements about the prior arrest were not directed toward the matter at issue. The transportation of controlled substance in a van in Florida was not a charged offense and was not material to any element of the actual charged offenses Petitioner was facing that day.

2. The Court failed to balance the potential for undue prejudice against the probative value of the evidence. This constitutes an abuse of discretion which should not be allowed and is not simply harmless error, which sometimes occurs in cases of this kind.

3. Petitioner, after his arrest, was kept in solitary confinement for two weeks, then interrogated by an unknown, terrifying individual who refused to give his name. He was forced to tell his story over and over again, and if he refused, was denied food and water. Not only is this conduct unacceptable to suspects in custody, but it was particularly disturbing in this case. In his childhood, Petitioner had been repeatedly interrogated by his father over trivial matters of discipline and asked to repeat over and over again in minute detail whatever the situation was. He was kept in a locked room for 24 hours at a time without food or water. Subsequent to these experiences, which went on for many years, Petitioner was found to be suicidally depressed by a physician at the boarding school he attended and was sent home for 6 months supposedly for psychiatric treatment. None was provided by the father, but at that time, Petitioner was victimized in another way.

At a sports game he was attending while at home, he was given a small amount of LSD by a supposed friend.

"It is not my intention to provide a lengthy account of the chemical properties of LSD. Suffice it to say that it is now well-documented that lysergic acid raises the levels of the neurotransmitter serotonin in the brain. In cases of depression, it has been clinically shown that low levels of serotonin coexist with depression. Therefore, it is conceivable that, denied treatment from any other source, yet suffering from the debilitating effects of profound depression, Petitioner had stumbled across a substance whose effects alleviated his symptoms. Clearly this was a case of self-medicating, though unrecognized at the time.

Current research in a Swiss hospital, which has accepted Petitioner as a patient in its rehabilitation clinic for the chronically depressed, and which specifically used LSD as a mainstay of their treatment, has shown its positive medical value as well as other hallucinogenic substances, such as psilocybin. Unfortunately these substances still carry the same stigma as cocaine or heroin in the public's estimation. *That is partly because of the CIA's early introduction of LSD into American society as part of a clandestine experiment in behavior modification and control, and then its subsequent attempts to cover up its role.*

"Pardon me, counsel," the Israeli judge interrupted. "What was the name of that clandestine operation? Did it have a name? Do you have that information?"

"Yes, your Honor. It did have a name. *The operation was known as MK-ULTRA.* As I stated, its purpose was to learn via experimentation, the properties of LSD on human being, so that the CIA would then have the knowledge to modify human behavior by cover means, if necessary."

"Are you saying, counsel, "the same judge persisted, "that the U.S. Intelligence Agency participated in experimentation on its own unwitting citizens with a dangerous drug without their consent?"

"That's exactly what I am saying, Your Honor," Jonathon stated

Cameras began flashing and reporters rushed to phones. A loud uproar by the visitors in the court eclipsed the judge, who kept shouting: "Order in the court! Order in the court!"

"May I continue?" Jonathon said, in perfect control.

"By all means."

"The CIA gave LSD *to innocent American adults and students in the San Francisco area and other places in the U.S. as part of MK-ULTRA.* It did not occur to the intelligence researchers to study any possible therapeutic use of LSD because that was not their purpose.

Those studies were subsequently done by psychologists, among them Dr. Timothy Leary while he was at Harvard. Of course, after 1962, no legal LSD was available and in 1968 former President Lyndon Johnson passed a Crime Bill specifically to halt any further legal experimentation with LSD, and as we can now surmise, also to cover up the CIA's involvement in MK-ULTRA."

"Of course, it was too late. A new, easily synthesizable drug had been unleashed upon the American people by its own government. Progressively harsher sentences for people using or selling LSD were enacted as the drug proliferated. The current average sentence is 20 to 40 years with no change of parole.

"Think of a young, 19 year old who, one night at a party, decides to experiment with LSD. The party is raided by the police, all the LSD is confiscated, and he is tried and sentenced to 20 years in prison. He would be released when he's about 40 years old. Am I the only person here who regards such punishment for this illegal act as both brutal and uncivilized?"

Jonathon paused, to let that last comment register. The courtroom was in a state of utter silence as he continued. "Compare that sentence to the one that rapists and murders get, on average 2 to 7 years, with the possibility of parole within a few months. But because the public had been manipulated into an irrational fear of drug, addiction, suicide, and a host of other horror associated with LSD, they continued to vote for harsher and harsher sentences, thinking they were getting rid of the problem."

"That policy was a failure, as we all know today. America's prisons are filled to the brim with nonviolent, first-time offenders who only crime was taking a sensational drug. They were not selling it, they were not stealing it, they were not shooting or hurting anyone. Yet their lives were, in good part, taken away from them. It took many years for the irrational sentencing for LSD offenses to be quietly altered so that it was be more on a par with sentences for drugs like marijuana."

"Unfortunately for my client, much of the world follows, and I would add, distantly, the example of the United States in many way.

One of them is the de facto copying of the U.S. penal code with one alteration: it is usually harsher. That is why my client received a 20 year sentence which is based on the old now-outdated in the U.S. mandatory minimum sentencing guidelines which are still in effect in the countries of Israel and Palestine."

"However, your Honors, my point today is not that Michael Bateson was harshly sentenced. My point is that he is innocent and was falsely charged. The proof of his being a participant in a so-called "drug deal" in the making at the Swap-Meet that day was in the form of his identification by two witnesses. The first witness' testimony is no longer salient. I will show why in a moment. The second witness' testimony is also inadmissable. He is an Israeli who belongs to a conservative religious sect, whose only argument against the Petitioner's alleged behavior was that it was in fact occurring on the Sabbath."

"On cross-examination, he contradicted himself several times, but the main disqualifying point was his continued focus on what he considered the crime to be: selling on the Sabbath. He never testified as what he thought Michael Bateson was supposedly selling. It was the selling itself which is what he designated a crime. I think that, giving due respect to all religious points of view, that this particular line of reasoning has no merit, if only because my client is not Jewish. Consequently he does not adhere to the same beliefs as the witness, whatever their ethical merit may be, and thus he cannot be considered having committed a crime."

"I will now discuss the first witness. She testified that she saw Michael Bateson in the presence of Wally Wausau before, during, and after the alleged attempt to sell drugs to another member of her tourist group. That person refused to testify. Petitioner denied being at the scene until he returned from lunch to find his friend Wally being beaten up by the police. The woman, an American tourist by the name of Clara Edstrom, was part of a Christian traditionalist group on a trip called "Pilgrimage Gala to the Holy Land". Clara had prepared herself for this trip for an entire year by memorizing biblical passages and attending religious lectures five times a week. She saturated herself with religious thinking. She knew by heart every winding turn on the Via Dolorosa. For Clara, it was the trip of her lifetime."

"After Michael and Wally had been arrested and Clara gave her statement to the police, she returned to the shopping district known as Jebel Mukaber in Jerusalem, just before the shops closed. Only, this time she looked entirely different than she did at the Swap-Meet. In fact, an entire transformation had taken place in her dress, in her demeanor, and most importantly, in her thinking. She wore a vibrant, multi-colored hooded robe and carried a large matching sack. According to the Jerusalem Post the next day, and verified by legal records which I have in my possession, she wandered into Ali Nuri's infant shop and began putting items from the shelves into her sack without paying for them. When Mr. Nuri, the proprietor, asked her what she was doing, she had a psychotic episode during which she began talking in tongues and striking Mr. Nuri repeatedly. Mr. Nuri's assistant telephoned Dr. Yair Bar-In, a well-known psychiatrist and physician in the area, who arrive in an ambulance within a few minutes and took Clara to the Kfar Shom Hospital where she is still recovering from her diagnosis of 'Jerusalem Syndrome.'

I have documentation on this condition, but suffice it to say at this time that medical opinion is such that Clara would be considered to have been in the grips of a psychotic episode that day, which had culminated in her outbreak at the shop a short time after her encounter at the Swap-Meet. It is not possible to pinpoint the exact moment when Clara lost touch with reality, but one can certainly entertain the notion that it might have begun even before she went to Ali's Shoppe."

"I wish to put forward my objection, therefore, to Clara Edstrom's competence as a witness against my client, based on the provable fact that she was experiencing a temporary psychosis at the time of the purported crime. Also, lest the prosecution anticipate a later motion calling other witnesses to the crime, let me remind the court of the protection to my client against double jeopardy."

"In closing, it is reasonable to assume that my client, instead of being an international drug dealer, as the prosecution would have us believe, was instead an innocent bystander. His past involvements with drugs, which are inadmissable as evidence anyway, did not have any relevance to the charges we are discussing today. I also wish to record the protest of Petitioner toward the joint governments of Israel and Palestine concerning his treatment while in custody in what is called the Neutral Trade Zone in the city of Jerusalem. It may be a place where people can be neutral in terms of taxes on imported goods, but it cannot be a place where people can be neutral to police brutality."

On that note, the treat of litigation for damages caused by police brutality, Jonathon ended his appeal. As the court recessed, he knew that a mistrial would be declared, and he could leave the details to the local attorneys for Michael Bateson. At this moment, all he kept thinking was how grateful he was for those alpha waves. He hardly looked at his notes, which is why his presentations were so successful. He knew that they were impeccable. He had done his homework, staying up most of the night drinking protein milkshakes while reading McIntyre's instructions and formulae. Good old McIntyre! Fortunately he hardly relied on the physiological medical analysis. It occupied only a small part of his argument, but it was correct in every detail. He must make a point to stop at the Centers for Disease Control in Atlanta, where McIntyre was now entrenched, to thank him. But, given his gregariousness, Jonathon knew that his planned one night visit would probably be stretched to a week. McIntyre does not like his hospitality to be turned down.

"Mr Miracle! Mr. Miracle!" Oh, no, Jonathon thought, the Press. He was in no mood to confront them now. They would be all over him asking questions about MK-ULTRA, he knew. Yet, there did not seem to be a way out. Where was that clever taxi driver when he needed him? Then he turned to face an angry, red-faced PSYCOPS, who whispered to him threateningly, "You dared to mention MK-ULTRA!"

A reporter, bolder than the rest, stuck a microphone up to Jonathon's face and shouted, "Are you publicly stating that the United States Intelligence Agency, the CIA, introduced LSD to hapless citizens under the guise of a covert experiment? Do I understand that to be your thoughts, sir?"

"That is EXACTLY what I am saying," Jonathon responded, just as boldly. PSYCOPS looked as if he were in the final throes of food poisoning.

"But you don't need me for this information, " Jonathon continued, undeterred. "Read a book called *Acid Dreams*, written by two of your journalist colleagues, if you haven't already. I'd be happy to do an interview sometime later. But right now, I have a plane to catch. Good day, gentlemen." Jonathon displayed what, in this part of the world, was called "chutzpah." He felt a card in his hand and glanced up to see an Art Buchwald-looking character. The card read, "*The Herald Tribune*." The Buchwald-look alike blurted out, "I'll meet you anywhere for that interview. Or just mail me your written thoughts to that address." He pumped Jonathon's hand several times.

The other journalists were in hot pursuit as Jonathon spotted Omar and his dilapidated taxi with its antiquated speakers blaring verbal sentimentalia from popular Arab vocal stars. Getting out of the car and immediately taking charge, her ushered Jonathon into the back seat, which had a still-burning cigarette in the ashtray. Omar literally came to blows with some of the more aggressive press, enjoying it all the while. What great stories he will have to tell his friends at the café!

"Omar, thank God you're here," Jonathon blurted out.

"Insha'allah, Insha'allah," he replied humbly.

"I've got to be at the airport as soon as possible, Omar."

"Of course, Habib! We go to the airport now."

And so they did, speakers blaring, leaving a group of disgruntled journalists and one happy and expectant editor from *The Herald Tribune* in their wake.

CHAPTER FOUR

Los Angeles

"Well, one less thing to think about," Jonathon sighed as he boarded an Air Palestine plane out of Jerusalem, bound non-stop for Los Angeles. "At last," he thought, "I can be anonymous again, and pampered, too," as he accepted a cool glass of champagne offered to him by the flight attendant. He looked down at the card in his hand. He felt a great affection for *The Herald Tribune* since he visited Paris many years ago. He remembered reading that international paper at the American Student Union on the Boulevard Raspail. After a long hiatus, here it was, back in circulation again. His affection for the newspaper prompted him to take out his tape recorder and begin a tape:

"You asked me for an interview. Here it is. I intend to put this case behind me as soon as I can, so you will not be able to reach me in the future on this issue. I do want to say at the outset that MK-ULTRA really isn't the issue, but read *Acid Rain* anyway. What is very important now is the judicial lag all over the world in terms of the positive, humanitarian changes in sentencing and prison policies, which took years and a great deal of effort to put into place in the United States. I am sorry to say, however, that there are still place there which are just as backward as many Third World countries insofar as prison philosophy goes. I am speaking of Texas first of all and then California, where I live. I can tell you that the composition of the prison population there does not reflect many individuals with an income of over $50,000. Most people who can afford to hire decent attorneys don't end up in prison.

The poorer you are, the higher you can expect your sentence to be, as a general rule."

"What will emerge in these third world countries? Certainly not Western homogeneous liberal democracy, but a more pragmatic view created by the merge of various philosophies and religious dogma."

Jonathon could not suppress a huge yawn. "Sorry, old boy," he dictated into the tape, "I'm going to sleep. Catch you later." Sound asleep moments later, Jonathon missed dinner and the movie. During a fitful sleep, he dreamt that he was lying in a recumbent position on the left side of a four lane highway. Glancing up from this prone position, he saw an ambulance about 10 miles away racing toward him. It was in the outermost left lane. He realized that in order to avoid being hit by the ambulance, he should roll his body over quickly to the right, but at that moment he saw another vehicle bearing down on him at the same speed and distance as the ambulance. His predicament was he was losing precious time oscillating in a decision whether to turn to the left or to the right. He decided to move haphazardly, taking his chances, but to his horror, he discovered that try as he might, he was unable to budge.

Panic began to overwhelm him. He kept thinking about how he had to make himself turn somehow, and that even if he succeeded, a part of him would be destroyed either direction he took. He squirmed, writhed, and constantly adjusted his position in his seat on the plane to Los Angeles, dreaming the same nightmare over and over again. Finally, he awoke with a start, totally drained emotionally.

The first thing he heard was a voice on the intercom: "Is there a Doctor on board? Is there a Physician on board? If so, please push your call button so that the flight attendant can locate you." He looked out the window and realized that they were on the final approach to Los Angeles. Couldn't they wait until the plane was on the ground in 30 minutes or so? What was the emergency? He decided to simply ask a passing flight attendant.

"Are you a physician?" she asked immediately, her face full of concern.

"No. I'm a lawyer. My only claim to medicine is 2 years of med school, but what I wanted to ask . . ." He was cut short by the flight attendant's boldly unbuckling his seat belt herself and lifting him up by the arm to lead him to the coach cabin.

"We haven't found any else on board. Please, " she implored.

"Well, I'll do what I can, which isn't much," Jonathon replied, a little alarmed.

"There's a woman in the coach cabin who seems very ill, in some sort of coma, so we can't communicate with her. We've called the paramedics at LAX, but in the meantime, the other passengers are panicking. We've put her in a vacant row. Follow me."

Jonathon wobbled down the aisle, having spent some 8 hours in one position dreaming about ambulances and trucks running him down on a deserted highway. Someone passed him a cup of black coffee which he consumed gratefully. He felt a sense of deja vu, with all eyes of the passengers on him, just like he was stared at in the courtroom in Jerusalem a short time ago.

Before he could react, he saw her. She was a middle-aged women who was having some sort of mild seizure, at first guess. Her eyes were unfocused pupils dilated. She was drooling. He sat down beside her and took her hand to feel her pulse. Her skin was clammy and cold. He dreaded the thought which came immediately to his mind, that this woman would be dead before they landed. The first interpretation which he thought of was a severe drug overdose. In fact, he couldn't get the idea out of his mind as the plane tipped downward on its final approach to the runway.

"Jonathon," he thought, "you've been working on too many drug cases lately. Your thinking is becoming reductionistic. Everyone is on drugs, you think, drugs are everywhere. Force yourself to think of another possibility. This woman's life could be saved."

Try as he might, the thought, "drug overdose" kept overriding the other contending diagnoses: stroke, heart attack, epilepsy, diabetic coma. Landing finally, the paramedics rushed on board while the rest of the passengers sat frozen, transfixed, motionless and terrified.

"Every passenger's nightmare," one of the paramedics commented without looking at Jonathon. They started an IV and oxygen flowing. Then, before the shock of being a witness to such a bizarre situation diminished, they whisked the still unconscious woman off the plane on a stretcher. It was the longest 30 minutes that Jonathon had ever spent in his life.

"Jonathon Miracle. Attorney," Jonathon answered the policeman's questions quickly. He was exhausted and wanted to get home, take a shower, and relax with a glass of iced scotch. He did ask to which hospital the women would be taken to, without thinking why he wanted to know. As far as he was concerned, he had enough excitement to last at least a year.

Eight hours later, he was on the phone to St. John's Hospital in Santa Monica. Yes, the emergency case had come in late last night. Then, abruptly and without explanation, he was transferred to another phone. A deep voice answered: "Lieutenant Moore."

"Lt. Moore, my name is Jonathon Miracle. I was on the plane yesterday from Jerusalem and witnessed the lady in shock. I was just wondering how she was and if I could be of any assistance."

"Well, Mr. Miracle, all I can tell you is that the case has been placed under the jurisdiction of the State Department," Moore answered.

"What? The State Department! What branch?"

"International narcotics."

"Lieutenant. Moore, I need to speak to you right away. I'll come there. I'm an attorney."

It was another beautiful day in Santa Monica. Seventy degrees and sunny, as usual. It was always heavenly in California so long as there were no earthquakes, mudslide, triple murders, or riots.

"Right this way," the young, efficient looking nurse smiled at Jonathon. Moore turned immediately as the door opened and Jonathon walked in.

"What do you know about Sylvia Grieg?" Moore said without offering a hello.

"Well, now I know that is the name of the woman on the plane. Other than that, nothing at all."

"You say you're an attorney?"

"Yes. I was returning from Israel and Palestine and happened to be on the same plane as this woman."

"Are you Michael Bateson's attorney?" Lt. Moore asked, then, continued without waiting for an answer, "Congratulations! I was just reading about you in the *L. A. Times*," Moore continued. "Perhaps, given who you are, I can be a little open about this case."

"By all means."

"No problem. It seems that the person in custody, Sylvia Grieg, was, we strongly suspect, a key link in an international drug smuggling ring whose origins were in Cairo, and whose trail went through Israel, and then on to Los Angeles. Ms. Grieg, we assume, had ingested some of the drug she was smuggling."

"Which drug was that?"

"LSD. In fact, we think her symptoms match a drug-induced psychosis with physical manifestations. When she recovers, if she ever does, she'll be charged with international drug trafficking, a sentence for which is . . ."

"Thirty years," Jonathon finished. "But what evidence do you have other than your hunches, Lieutenant?"

"We found some pretty incriminating evidence too," Moore answered.

"Like?"

"Like a notebook with writing in it matching her signature on her passport. She kept a lot of detailed notes about names and so forth, some which seem to be people in Egypt and others in the United States. But the really incriminating thing are the formulas that she meticulously wrote out. The chemists here say they are the chemical diagrams for LSD and MDMA."

"So you think her source was Egypt?" Jonathon continued.

"Yes, although LSD and MDMA can be made here, so that

part doesn't make sense. But it still could be possible. She had tickets for future trips stashed away in her purse. She lived in a one room apartment in Santa Monica and was behind in her rent. She had no money on her whatsoever, and we can't find any record of relatives or family. We're going to appoint an attorney to start investigating, though."

"You don't have to do that, Lieutenant. She already has an attorney," Jonathon heard himself stating.

"Oh yeah? Who?" Moore asked suspiciously.

"Me. You're looking at him." Jonathon took one of the copies of the notebook from the lieutenant and gave him his card. Walking home, which wasn't far, he began feeling annoyed and agitated. Something wasn't right. He thought about the last 72 hours. A route from Cairo to Jerusalem to Los Angeles for a drug which can be manufactured in the United States? It didn't make sense. Details of Michael Bateson's case came into his awareness. LSD. He was becoming angry with himself. Why didn't he arrive in Jerusalem earlier so that he could have interviewed Bateson and Wausau directly? He could have had an intuitive feel for them had he done that.. Instead, he took the word of the CIA as if it were gospel and didn't think twice about it, all the while complaining at the appeal about sloppy thinking!

Coincidences like this just don't happen. It was becoming very clear to Jonathon that Michael Bateson, Wally Wausau, and Sylvia Grieg were all part of a larger drug ring which the CIA had known about all along but about which they did not inform Jonathon. He had been duped. Now he understood the twinkle in PSYCOPS' eyes at his insincere reprimand at Jonathon's bringing up MK-ULTRA.

Jonathon thought to himself, "First you don't get anything, and now you are leaping to far-fetched conclusions. Slow down, Miracle." He couldn't wait to get home to call Washington, hoping that PSYCOPS had returned from what must have been a victory celebration with his sleazy partners. Passing a newspaper stand with foreign journals displays, he spotted his own photograph alongside that of Omar's in an Italian paper, the caption reading: "Miracle: Capo Di Tutti Capi". The truth was, he was more like the whore of the CIA. Omar was probably part of it all along, Omar and his feigned obsequiousness. What a setup, Jonathon thought with disgust.

They're not finished with me yet, Jonathon hissed between clenched teeth as he dialed the CIA.

"PSYCOPS. This is Miracle."

"Good Lord, Jonathon, how ARE you?"

"Are you still stewing about my mentioning MK-ULTRA?"

"What? Oh, that. Well, let's call it an indiscretion. But probably harmless. I hope no one reads *Acid Dreams*, though. A lot of damaging stuff in there. I doubt it though, since the CIA tried to destroy all the copies of it we could find. Outside of that unpleasant topic, I never did get to congratulate you on your brilliant appeal."

It was all too hypocritical, thought Jonathon.

"Thanks. Glad there's no hard feelings. I wanted to tell you that I have a new client. A very strange case. A women became unconscious on the same plane I was on returning from Jerusalem to L.A."

"Really! How strange. Well, " PSYCOPS mused, "I suppose one can pick up a client almost anywhere these days!"

"Her name is Sylvia Grieg," Jonathon stated, then waited for a reaction.

PSYCOPS paused, then finally said, "So?"

"Well, I thought you might have heard about her. She's under the jurisdiction of the International Division."

"Hmm. Well. Good luck with that. I have to go. Stay in touch."

"Sure." It was all Jonathon could do to restrain himself. PSYCOPS must think I am a complete idiot, he thought. I must be the laughingstock of the entire CIA. They all knew about this clever drug trio.

The darker side of Jonathon's imagination began fomenting. "They are probably part of it." He recalled the first evening when he had heard of the assignment. He had been sitting next to a so-called cultural ecologist at a Washington dinner who used the term "promiscuous altruist." With an increasing sense of self-disgust, Jonathon realized exactly that he embodied the term.

Enough hand-wringing, he thought. Time to get busy.

Jonathon took the copy of Sylvia Grieg's notebook. It looked fairly ordinary. Could be an executive planner. Upon opening it, however, he was confronted with a mass of detail, replete with drawings and formulas, just as Lt. Moore had described. There were also phone numbers and addresses which seemed to be in Egypt, Palestine and Israel. The formulas were intriguing. He took out his old chemistry text from medical school and compared several codes. He found a formula in the notebook for aspirin, then nicotine. These seemed benign enough. Then, as he turned a few more pages, there they were, in full detail, the chemical notation for crack and LSD.

"We know so little about the brain," he remembered Dr. McIntyre expounding, "but what we *can* say with some measure of certainty is that our brain contains receptors for every drug which can affect us. That means that we are capable of producing them ourselves. Think about it. In that respect, we are all on holding."

Jonathon refocused on the notebook, finding long pages of notes about the roles of serotonin, dopamine, and acetylcholine, all neurotransmitters which are vital for every aspect of our functioning. He continued turning pages. Chemical terms were scattered about like editorial notes on a manuscript. Then, something puzzling.

Secretum Meum Mihi Est

A Latin phrase. He thought for a few minutes, then said aloud, "my secret is my own." Why would Sylvia Grieg write that in her notebook otherwise filled with chemical notations? Since she was on a respirator, he couldn't ask her. The jumble of drug formulas and terms signified what? Was she a chemist who synthesized illicit drugs in a laboratory somewhere in the world? If so, where?

Los Angeles? Cairo? Palestine? Israel? What if she died before he learned her story? Jonathon reasoned that if she stayed unconscious for two to three days, which seemed likely, he could do a fair amount of investigating, but according to his terms this time.

One of his first tasks was to reconstruct Sylvia's trip from the addresses listed in the notebook. There were first names alongside the addresses in Cairo. In order to make any sense of this growing conspiracy, he needed to make contact with these sources. That meant Egypt.

CHAPTER FIVE

Cairo

Armed only with Sylvia's notes and his own intuition, Jonathon left for Cairo the next day, oblivious to the effects which cumulative jet lag might have on his system. At least his frequent flier airline points would be accumulating exponentially, he thought sarcastically. To entertain himself he brought along two books by the guru of chemistry in the modern age, the late Dr. Sidney Cohen, who had been one of Jonathon's early heroes. Dr. Cohen's impeccable reputation and vast knowledge about drugs made him an invaluable asset in the confrontation with the conservative, anti-treatment, pro-incarceration groups in the United States, who he liked to say preferred to remain ignorant rather than to face their fears and prejudices. It was from this mentality that the support for the progressively harsher sentences for drug offenses had sprung.

Time sped by as always when Jonathon was engrossed in reading material which was not required for a case nor the trade publications peculiar to the academic specialities. He looked forward to dinner, more reading, then sleep. Arrival at Cairo Airport would be very late at night and Jonathon opted to stay at a hotel close to the airport that night. He was hoping the concierge might be able to locate a driver as talented and ingenious as Omar was.

The hotel seemed luxurious after the crush of people, the noise, the confusion of Cairo Airport. He allowed himself to wake up naturally and after a typical protein-packed Egyptian breakfast, rumored to provide enough energy to conduct the day's business and most of the evening's social obligations (of which in Cairo there were many), he faced the prospects of this new day over bland Sanka coffee and an early edition of *Al Ahram*.

"Good morning, Mr. Miracle!" Jonathon looked up to see a concierge disguised as a military commander, or maybe it was the other way around.

"I have a driver for you! Here . . ." he lingered, pointing to his right side to the figure standing there, "is Ali." The man he motioned to wore the standard Middle Eastern service class uniform, a pima cotton sport shirt with the ubiquitous cigarettes (preferable American for snob value) stuffed in one pocket and a ball point pen to note important message with, in the other; tan cotton wrinkled and slightly stained slacks with a belt pulled too tightly, sandals with huge leather straps, and to complete the costume, a shiny quartz imitation Rolex watch which was capable of displaying the time on three continents.

"Good morning Sir!" Ali energetically and loudly spoke, while gesticulating needlessly with his hands. "I can take you all day, anywhere, same price. How are you?"

Jonathon was fast-becoming accustomed to this strange, out-of-sequence parlance spoken by many Arabs whose English was functional in the practical sense, but whose flow was staccato-like and whose shifts in temporal nuance disconcerting. He was also becoming pleasantly aware of a sense of safety, very subtle, in the presence of those Arabs to whom he entrusted himself. He questioned whether he was simply deluding himself, or feeling the aggregate effects of jet lag. Yet he could not deny that while in the company of these service people, Middle Eastern drivers, concierges, restauranteurs and store owners, Jonathon felt protected from any harm which might be lurking in the immediate vicinity. Whether genuinely or not, Jonathon embraced the sense of warmth and trust he felt with Ali, who would become his eyes and ears during his stay in Egypt.

"Uh. Let's see. Ali, can you take me to 50 Abd el Aziz Street in Maadi? Thank you. No, thank you. I don't smoke." Jonathon smiled in spite of himself. He was beginning to like Egypt.

"Do you speak any arabic? Yes? A good accent. Maadi? This is a long way, but it is a good place, safe, with comfortable hotels. Very cheap and good. First time to Cairo? A wonderful city!" Ali went on reciting his tourist stories in the same non-sequitur fashion which Jonathon had come to expect, all the while eyeing him in the rear view mirror, sizing him up, with a totally objective look on his worn, dark face. Ali changed subjects often, Jonathon thought on purpose, before he could answer, keeping control of the situation, as he swung his dilapidated Volvo onto the congested highway toward Maadi, the furthermost suburb from the city proper before reaching the road leading to the pyramids.

"American, yes?" Again, without waiting for a reply, Ali continued. "Good time for you to drive, in the morning. You will see all of Cairo. How it *really* is. Music?"

This time Jonathon didn't object. Ali was so pleased to play his "American" tapes of rock groups which Jonathon had never heard of and soon, windows down all the way, radio blaring, they were in the midst of the teeming metropolis itself. Cars whizzed by the numerous pedestrians who seemed oblivious to them as they lumbered alongside and at times across the busy highway, some with pots balanced on their heads, others with babies strapped to their backs, but each one with an expression of eternal resignation on their ageless faces. Quite unlike the sharp alertness of the Palestinians. That hyper-alertness, Jonathon surmised, was probably due to the effect of living under virtual military occupation for decades. He contemplated the cumulative impact of free-floating, constant anxiety on an entire society like the Palestinians. Never knowing when a shot will ring out, when another neighbor will be dragged away for questioning and detention.

But here in Cairo, such a sense of friction was absent. People, dogs and cars were everywhere without that sense of imminent danger perceptible in places like Palestine or New York. Perpetual motion. Brightness bristling as the constant movement of heads, shoulders, and bodies began anew with the daybreak in this eternal city. Every sense of Jonathon's being was stimulated by the continuous bombardment of color, the muted sounds of distant music, the aroma of coffee, roasting meat smothered with spices, the tactile assault of people upon each other with their arms, shoulders, and sometimes their backs and stomachs, as they shared previous space in buses, cars, and sometimes streets. Weaving a convoluted path through the density of people, animals, cars and bicycles, the old Volvo lurched unevenly along.

"Look! Mr. Jonathon, here to the left! You see? Saladin's wall. You know Saladin, yes?"

"Well," Jonathon drawled, "I think I remember a little about him in history class."

This was the opening Ali had been waiting for. "Saladin-a great warrior!" he began. "In his most famous battle, surrounded by enemies, with no escape possible for him and his beautiful black stallion, except to jump over that wall."

"Really!" Jonathon knew that his sincerity would not unheeded. Yet he was not entirely focused on myths and stories about other men's actions centuries ago. There was too much at stake in the world of the present, the world of this particular moment. However, he humored Ali by listening to what turned out to be a very long tale, during which, sometime in the middle of the telling, Ali's eyes actually shone with tears. Finally, the Volvo turned sharply into an unremarkable street. Nothing seemed to distinguish it from any other avenue in the area. No signs, not even numbers. How had Ali found it? When he got out of the Volvo, however, Jonathon saw that he was in front of some sort of institution. He had expected a small, darkly-lit storefront-like affair, the place of contact for Sylvia Grieg and her comrades. In fact, this building looked remarkably like a school.

"Ali, are you sure this is the address I showed you?"

"Oh yes, no mistake! Ali makes no mistakes. Your hotel-is next door, right there. My good friend runs it and I will tell him about you so that he will take good care of you. Also, a good place to east roast squabs nearby."

Jonathon's style of thinking, usually analytical, was not

equipped to process the way information was packaged in Cairo-directions coupled with culinary suggestions all in the same sentence. "Great! Please wait for me here."

Jonathon walked stiffly, feeling his jet lag and anxiety coalescing, reaching the only door in sight and, finding it open, stepped inside a large vestibule with checked marble floors, black and white. In front of him stood an enormous dark oak staircase, very grand. He saw no one around and heard nothing. Turning left, he slowly walked down a long, dark and windowless hall, coming eventually to an administrative-looking office where he paused, peering inside. He earnestly hoped that the woman there, now regarding him curiously from behind an empty desk with a telephone and steno pad on it, would speak English.

"Uh, hellothereGrieg.G-R-I-E-G. Do . . .you . . .know . . .that . . .name?" He stammered clumsily, not knowing the identity of the woman standing in front of him. She rose from her chair, stretched herself to her full height, as if she was determined to be on exact eye level with him. Finally, she broke the almost unbearable silence, and speaking in perfect but clipped English, asked him to have a seat. She would return, she said. With whom or what? Jonathon though. He sat down on an uncomfortable wooden chair and stared at her coffee cup on the desk next to the phone, wondering if she drank the supposedly delectable Arabica coffee or the bland Nescafe or Sanka which was forever offered to him in the Middle East. The fan whirred. He wondered if Ali had driven off. He had a distinct urge to close his eyes, just for one minute, but fought against it.

Finally, a full thirty minutes later, another woman appeared, this one stern and middle-aged, matronly-looking with a white scarf all around her head. In all other respects, however, she was dressed in a typically middle-income Western business fashion. Perched on the tip of her nose was a pair of officious-looking tortoise shell rimmed glasses, attached on either end to a strap so as to remain on her chest suspended from her neck when not in use. She peered at Jonathon over the bifocals but did not introduce herself. Nor did she smile.

"La Grande Inquisitor," Jonathon thought.

"Your name?" The Inquisitor demanded abruptly.

"Miracle. Jonathon Miracle."

"Your purpose here?

"I am a friend of the family."

"You? You are a friend of the family?"

"Yes. Of the mother."

"The mother?" the Inquisitor stared at him over her bifocals.

She asked a lot of questions but offered no information in return, nor exuded any warmth, which seemed very odd for an Egyptian. Jonathon wished he had asked Ali to accompany him, but it was too late for that now. The questions continued.

"What is your business here? What do you want? Who sent you? Where are you staying? Who do you know in Egypt?" She was thorough enough, Jonathon though, probably trained by the Israeli authorities at Tel Aviv Airport, or the CIA.

He was becoming slightly annoyed. He was hot, tired, thirsty and discouraged. Yet he maintained a professional nonchalant manner similar to one he would display before an airport interrogation official. He had long ago learned to tolerate seemingly pointless interlocutions. Interactions such as this one, which appeared to be capricious at first, would make a great deal of sense later, after a wonderful shower and over a chilled glass of wine. His mind was wandering off to such pleasant thoughts. After twenty more minutes of irrelevant, staccato-like questions, even this non-smiling, bifocaled matron gave up with a plaintive sigh accompanied by incomprehensible grumbling in arabic.

"There is no one by that name here," she straightened up and declared.

"What?" Jonathon almost shouted back, thoroughly irritated now.

"I said . . ."

"Oh, never, mind. I understand. I do understand. This is a complete waste of time, " he replied, indifferent to his rudeness. After all, she did not even offer him a cup of arabic coffee.

The Inquisitor regarding him incomprehensibly for a moment, perfectly still, as if contemplating some sort of appropriate punishment. Then she suddenly turned, long skirts swooshing in the room's silence, and strode purposely down the hall, completely ignoring Jonathon who was left sitting in the monastic like room alone.

Why . . .is Cairo so . . .*hot?* He thought as he eased himself up from the uncomfortable wooden chair. He sluggishly walked out of the office, discouragement showing. Looking once more for the palatial entrance, suggestive more of a palace than a place of education, he smiled wryly as he once again encountered the younger, more sprightly woman who had first greeted him. She did not speak, but motioned him to follow her.

"You are looking for Grieg?" she said, almost whispering.

"Yes."

"Over there, " she replied, matter-of-factly, pointing to the garden within an atrium. Around a clockwatch tower in a distance Jonathon could make out the figure of a young woman walking with a boy.

"There. Can you see? There is Grieg," the young veiled woman said, mor emphatically now. Jonathon looked intently, squinting in the sunlight which was streaming unshielded through the tall windows, at the couple crossing the open space in the courtyard. When he turned, the young woman was gone, disappearing silently before he could ask her anything else or even thank her.

Jonathon found the door to the courtyard slightly ajar. He stepped through it onto the gravel and walked toward the young woman and boy. He had no idea what he would say, and simply blurted out: "Excuse me. I'm looking for a person named Grieg. Can you help me?"

"Who are *you?*" the young woman asked, feigning disinterest.

"My name is Jonathon Miracle. And who are you, if I may ask?"

The young woman looked up sharply, green eyes shining defiantly, and said boldly and clearly, "I am Mona Grieg-Huzam."

"Oh . . .I am so pleased to meet you," Jonathon replied in total shock. "And . . .your are?" Jonathon moved toward the boy, about 16 years old, who had been walking beside Mona.

"I'm Tarif," he said spontaneously. A ill-disguised whiff of suspiciousness was in the air.

"You are probably wondering why I am here," Jonathon began tentatively. "I have recently met a lady by the name of Sylvia Grieg. I understand that you may . . ."

Jonathon had no choice by to pause in face of the change in the young woman's demeanor which had become hyper-vigilant. "What do you have to do with her?"

"I am her attorney," Jonathon stated, looking at Mona Grieg-Huzam squarely. He continued, "She is very ill in a hospital in Los Angeles and I need to find out about her, that's why I'm here. Perhaps you can help. It may mean the difference between life and death."

Tarif started to blurt out something. Mona quickly restrained him, putting her hand across his mouth while squeezing his arm tightly. Then she faced Jonathon.

"You can tell my mother that we do not need her, that her trick of playing sick to get us to contact her won't work, that we are quite fine here without her, and that she need not bother herself about us, and that she need not come here again."

"You mean she was here recently? Did you see her? If you are her children it is imperative that I speak to you about her. She needs you help," Jonathon was blurting out sentences awkwardly, like a reporter, he realized, but he was grasping at anything to keep Mona's attention and interest.

"Go away and leave us alone. To us, our mother is dead. Come on, Tarif, we have to go home."

Tarif lingered, looking uncomfortable and angry. Jonathon pulled out the card he had picked up from the hotel in Maadi which Ali had recommended. He quickly shoved it into Tarif's had.

"Remember my name: Miracle. I'll be here tonight. Call me,

or just come to the hotel. I'll be waiting for you," Jonathon whispered desperately.

Tarif shoved the card into his jeans, turned abruptly and walked off without saying a word. They did not look back. There was nothing left now for Jonathon to do but to go to his hotel and wait. He instructed Ali to pick him up the following morning for the drive to the airport. He did not really expect anything to materialize from his encounter with the Grieg children. What would he say if the showed up? He wasn't really sure. He had traveled half way around the world without knowing what he was looking for and what he would do if he found it.

Still, questions lingered. Why did Sylvia Grieg have a drug reaction on the plane from Palestine to Los Angeles? Or was it just simple food poisoning? Perhaps there were no plots, no intrigue. Just a simple family feud, a divorce, and on the way back the mother was overcome. Maybe a suicide attempt by overdose. The entire scenario had been built upon the overreaction of the authorities in Los Angeles and had appealed to his overactive imagination. Not the first time for such a thing to happen, Jonathon thought. The "Idea Freak" as he was nicknamed in law school, who has just reached another dead end. Still, his curiosity remained piqued. Who was the husband-father, Huzam? Did the children live with him now? Why was Mona so hostile toward Sylvia? The least they could have done was to fill in the patchy story he had contrived about their mother up to this point. Why did she write such odd things in her notebook? Was she a nurse? Why did Huzam and Sylvia divorce, if indeed they did? How long ago did this happen? How did this affect the children?

The questions plagued him endlessly. He could never take a fact at face value. His imagination was always expanding it, a habit of extreme irritation to most legal minds who go strictly by the facts. He ordered dinner brought to his room and afterward resumed his obsessive theorizing, although even he was getting weary of this one-way barrage of all questions and no answers. At about 10 P.M., there was an abrupt knock on his door.

"Yes?"

"It's Tarif."

Jonathon opened the door immediately. There stood a typical gangly 16 year old youth. He looked quite the part, half-German, half-Egyptian, with brown curly hair and dark eyes. Strong looking. But there was something which was deeply disturbing him.

"What do you know about my mother?" Tarif stated straightforwardly without any polite conversation preceding his query.

"I have seen her. She is in a hospital in Los Angeles. She is very ill, but will probably be all right."

"What is the matter with her?"

"Well, that's hard for me to say, as she was unconscious when I left her and the doctors and nurses did not have a clear idea. It may be food poisoning, something she ate while she was here or one the plane. If that's all it is, she's in good hands and will be okay in a couple of days. When did you see her last?"

"A couple of days ago. We had dinner at a restaurant in the Moqqattam Hills, near the Citadel. Do you know it? It's a popular tourist place, near Saladin's Wall."

"I've heard of it," Jonathon said, recalling the conversation with his driver Ali.

"Are you sure my mother is going to be okay?" Tarif asked tentatively, his earnest eyes searching Jonathon's face.

"I have no doubt that she will be fine in a couple of days," Jonathon said completely without any basis, "and I will be seeing her soon, when I return to L.A. Is there any message I can give her from you?"

"Give her this." Tarif handed Jonathon a plain white folded envelope.

"She'll know it's from me," he said without emotion.

"Okay. You can count on me to get it to her. You have my word." Jonathon looked at Tarif intently.

"I have to go now," Tarif said reluctantly.

"But when can I see you again? When can we talk longer?" Jonathon replied hopefully.

"When are you leaving?" Tarif asked as he turned toward the door.

"Probably tomorrow, but I can delay my departure. Can we meet before I leave?"

Tarif did not reply but looked uneasy. He started to say something but stopped short. Jonathon felt uncomfortable putting pressure on this adolescent who was obviously in a difficult situation. "Don't worry. I'm not the police or anything like that. I was just a passenger on the same plane as your mother. The one from Palestine to Los Angeles. She got very sick and I helped her. That's all. I saw her in the hospital yesterday."

Tarif looked anxious and somewhat impulsively, he blurted out, "I have to go now. I'm late. Be sure to give that to my mother."

"Wait!" Jonathon shouted as Tarif darted out the door and bolted down the hall. "Come back tomorrow. I'll be here waiting," he blurted out as he ran after the boy, who had disappeared before Jonathon reached the stairs. He had completely vanished into the Egyptian night by the time Jonathon reached the front desk. He walked slowly back to his room. Ali was arriving early the next morning, and he had to pack. He would not have time to locate the Huzam household at this late hour, and what would he do if he did? What sort of person was Mr. Huzam? Probably, following another hunch, Jonathon mused that Huzam would become angry, why this intrusion? He doubted that he would hear from Tarif again, much less Mona. The information they had provided brought a small amount of rationality to the convoluted and complex situation of personalities and events. Still he had not made complete sense of it all. He had to face the fact that he had probably gone on one of his wild goose chases, whose only foundation was a hunch.

"You have to stop living on ideas," he heard his father's voice commanding him, as he had often during his formative years. "The *Dreamer* of the family," the old man would remark with resignation, but not without a little pride. Years ago he remembered that quality of creative imaginative thinking, which he once had in abundance but which had since quietly faded away due to the practical exigencies of making a living, surviving, and raising his children.

Jonathon turned off the dim lights in the room wondering what effect his encounter would have on Sylvia's children. As far as she was concerned, once she recovered from food poisoning, she would face the exaggerated and flimsily supported charges of the L.A. prosecutor, known to be overly zealous, and be acquitted of the charge of drug conspiracy, because of lack of evidence. Jonathon would not mind at all representing her as he had stated he would to Lieutenant Moore. Then his life would settle into the complacent orderly schedule he had created for himself on the West Coast. He looked forward to the reassuring predictability of his life, as he sat in the lonely and now rather cold hotel room in the middle of Cairo.

"I came all the way over here for nothing," his conscience reprimanded. He allowed himself to take the full emotional impact of unmitigated guilt for his circumstances. He had spent a lot of money on a last-minute plane ticket which could have been spent on better things. Before the self-bashing continued, Jonathon thought he would break the spell of defeat which was insidiously being created around him by his own mind by taking a shower.

Unbuttoning his shirt, he felt the crinkle of a paper in his pocket. Tarif's note. He unfolded it and held it under the dim Egyptian light. He read:

> "For all these years I've not been here
> because I have a chronic fear
> that being in the present tense
> would strip me of my last defense
> against the terror known as "Life"
> which I have found to be too rife
> with anguish, heartbreak and despair
> for any feeling soul to bear.
> Thus I have kept myself apart,
> pretended that I have no heart,

avoided being too awake,
and searched for ways that I could fake
a pseudo-personality
concealed in much banality
to deftly substitute in lieu
of really being here with you.
I've gotten very good at this,
and only dimly do I miss
the warmth that other people feel
who have the courage to be real..
I think my way of life is best,
and so I make this firm request:
Don't wake me up, don't make me see
my triumph is a . . .tragedy."

Jonathon stared at the poem. He was astounded at Tarif's poetical dexterity, for only being sixteen, and he felt a pang of identification, a resonance, somewhere deep within him, with the meaning which the words expressed. An urgent sense of empathy for this lonely youth had developed and Jonathon did not realize why or what he was supposed to do about it. He preferred to remain uninvolved after he left tomorrow and after Sylvia's case was resolved.

But the poem had captured his imagination. His compassion for others was winning, despite his constant battle against those aspects of himself which his father had identified as "weak, undisciplined, and totally useless sentimentality". The emotional upheaval he was feeling exhausted him. After a shower he had another drink, a little stronger than usual, and slipped into bed thinking about the last refrain of Tarif's poem as he drifted into a fitful sleep: *my triumph is my tragedy*, he whispered.

It seemed only a short time later that Jonathon reluctantly found himself awake, wondering where he was. Jerusalem? Los Angeles? Cairo? The loud, repetitive knocking on the door brought him to his full senses. He looked at his watch. 8 A.M. He was in Maadi. Ali was probably making sure he would make it to the airport on time.

"I'll be right there, Ali."

"It's Mona Grieg."

Jonathon opened the door and beheld the lovely young woman who unselfconsciously stroke into the room and asked, "How about breakfast?"

Over coffee, Mona recited a long and obviously painful story involving the dissolution of her parents' long marriage and eventual divorce several years ago. "My mother was one of those traditional women who had devoted herself to the children in every way. She tried to be the perfect everything to everyone, including my father. But several years ago, she started to change."

"In what way?" Jonathon asked.

"Well, she began to become interested once again in the work she did before she married my Dad. And of course Tarif and I were getting older. We didn't need so much of her time."

"What work?"

"Physiologic psychology. She did research about brain chemicals."

"Like neurotransmitters?"

"How did you know that?"

"I was an unsuccessful medical student before I became a lawyer. I spent a lot of time studying neurotransmitters because one of my professors had a passion for them."

"Oh that's cool, so you must know all about synapses and agonists and inhibitors. Mom used to talk about those all the time while we were eating breakfast. It was her passion too."

"She must know a lot more than I do, because I became a lawyer not a doctor. But, go on."

"Well, my mother decided to get her Ph.D., as I was saying, about 5 years ago. She really wanted to make a contribution to humanity. It became an obsession. She became involved in research. But I wanted to ask you something. Was my brother here last night? He said you were some kind of miracle. I don't understand."

"My *name* is Miracle. Jonathon Miracle."

"Hmm. Strange name. Anyway, I was furious with Tarif for sneaking over here."

"Why?"

"Because. If my father had found out, he would have gotten a beating he would not have forgotten."

"Tell me about him later."

"Well, he's getting good lately at dodging my father and his demands that he take courses in school so that he can become a scientist like he is."

"Wait a minute," Jonathon thought suddenly. "Are you the family? I mean, a few years ago I read in the news about this scientist who ran away and left his family behind. Would that be your father?"

"Probably. Except the only he left behind was my mom. We were on television too."

"Yes. I remember. Your brother must have been about 4. How did you contact your mother after your father took you out of the country?"

"My father told us where she was living, because I wrote her and my letters were returned. He's a neurologist by the way. For some reason, we could not understand what happened between them, why he left her without any explanation. Instead, we were given strict rules never to discuss my mother or even to mention her name in front of him. Of course, my mother began investigating about where we were from the very start."

"And that angered your father."

"That's putting it mildly. It wasn't only about losing custody over us. That wasn't all there was to it. He wanted to keep my mother in the dark. He wanted to punish her, because he never forgave her for wanting to do something other than to direct all of her energy toward him and my brother and me. He couldn't accept the fact that he-and us-were not enough for her."

"And then . . .?"

"Then, one summer about six years ago . . ."

"How old were you then?"

"Sixteen."

"What happened?"

"One night Dad said we were going away on a vacation to Egypt, where he was born. We packed our things excitedly only thirty minutes before we were to be at the airport."

"What about your mother?"

"He said she was going to follow us. She was interning at a hospital that night and had not been home since the previous morning. We assumed that she knew all about it."

"Did your father let you assume that?"

"Yes."

"Didn't you realize that your parents were having problems? That maybe there was something suspicious about not talking about leaving before, that maybe it was your father's way of quitting a marriage without all the expense and trouble of the law, which probably would have favored your mother over him anyway."

Mona was silent for a long time. A sole tear trickled down her cheek. "Yes," she admitted. "It occurred to me. My father assured me that he had asked her to live with us in Egypt but that she had refused. He said that she told him that her work was more important to her than we were. He claimed that she was willing to give us up."

"And you believed him?"

"Yes. I believed him eventually, because she didn't follow us," Mona said loudly, defiantly, angrily. "Why wouldn't she come too? Why did she close us out of her life? I decided that I would close her off too. After a couple of years I heard from a friend who had seen her. He said that she had moved to California. She had always wanted to live there but my father was against it. He thought it was a bad place to raise children. My friend told me that things were pretty bad for her there. She had very little money. She had jobs which I would never take, like being a waitress, telemarketing. She couldn't afford a telephone in her room. She didn't have money to buy a plane ticket to see us. If she wrote, we never received any of her letters."

Mona paused. The strain of the conversation was beginning to show. Her face was contorted. It was a struggle for her to continue. She gazed at Jonathon for several minutes, then added, "Mr. Miracle, I can't talk about this anymore."

Jonathon felt moved by her honesty and by the trauma she had just described. "I understand," he said softly, putting a fatherly arm around her. "Listen, I'll be leaving Cairo for Los Angeles in about two hours. I should be there by tomorrow afternoon. I promise you that I will go directly to the hospital where your mother is staying and I will personally give her any message you have."

"Message?" Mona retorted. "I don't think you realize something, Mr. Miracle." She fumbled in her purse for moment and extracted a plane ticket. "I'm coming with you."

Within a few hours, Jonathon and Mona had left Maadi in Ali's taxi so that she could collect a few things for the trip. They arrived at the four-story concrete apartment building which had been their home for the last five years. Mona turned toward Jonathon and said, "Come on up while I pack. It's okay. My father and Tarif left for Iraq early this morning. They won't be back for a week."

"Iraq!"

"My dad goes there often on business trips," Mona added. "He works with some neurologists there. Once in a while he takes Tarif or me with him. He never stays longer than a week. I have got to be back here before he returns, though. He would kill me if he knew I had been to the United States with you to see my mother."

"He's not going to hurt anyone," Jonathon stated, noticing how easily frightened she became.

They climbed the stairway to the second floor of the building where the Huzams lived. It was a large, four bedroom apartment decorated in a sort of nondescript style, an unlikely combination of Louis XIV with Miami *kitsch*. Classic but vaguely tacky.

"Odd," Jonathon said aloud as he studied the photographs on

the wall in the living room, while Mona went to her room. There was a photograph of a young Sylvia Grieg with an infant, probably Tarif, pacifier in his mouth, together with a pensive, seven year old Mona. Then another, a serious, harsh-looking man in hospital greens. Hammad Huzam, Jonathon surmised, the father, standing in front of what looked like a military building of some sort. More photos of Sylvia with the children at different stages of their childhood. It looked happy.

Jonathon noticed than Hammad Huzam was never in a photo together with Sylvia. He wandered into a hallway which beckoned from the living room. Mona was in her bedroom opening and closing drawers and closet doors. He felt safe in exploring. The hall led to a pantry and kitchen, equipped with the bare basics but not more. No microwave, icemaker, disposal or trash compactor. Outdated, Jonathon thought, as he slowly opened the old-fashioned gas oven door.

"What?" Jonathon whispered under his breath as he found several petri dishes on the middle rack of the oven. He examined them carefully without disturbing them. He knew something about cultures, about how and why they are grown. Growing organisms in petri dishes is not something one forgets easily. Jonathon did not want to stop speculating on the reason petri dishes were there and what was growing inside of them, but he was acutely aware that Mona might walk in on him any moment. Was growing cultures routinely done at home in Egypt, if one were a practicing doctor? No, Jonathon thought, surely there must be some other explanation. Jonathon impulsively but carefully extricated one of the petri dishes from its place on the rack and placed it in his jacket pocket. He also took a vial filled with something black which had been on a tray next to the cultures in the oven. He put it into his pocket also.

As that moment Mona suddenly and without warning appeared in the kitchen. "I'm ready," she announced. Then looking ad Jonathon closely, she added, "What are you doing in the kitchen? Were you looking for something to drink? You can get awfully thirsty in Cairo. But the place to find a drink is in the refrigerator, not in the oven!" she laughed, reaching over and extracting a bottle of mineral water.

"Thanks," Jonathon answered, trying to sound nonchalant. "You're right. I was very thirsty," he added, closing the oven door carefully before turning around to face Mona.

The sound of a car revving could be heard distinctly from the kitchen window. "Ali," Jonathon said, picking up Mona's bags. They went down to the taxi. "We've got to get to the airport quickly."

Ali laughed good naturedly as if given a challenge at a sports event. Then he pushed down hard on the gas pedal. He showed himself to be a virtuoso at driving in Cairo that morning, weaving in and out of lanes at opportune moments, honking his horn constantly, radio blasting, windows wide open, and cigarette dangling precariously on his lower lip. Jonathon winced as he turned to Mona.

"It's Omm Khalsum," she said, smiling slightly.

"What's that?" Jonathon shouted above the din of the traffic.

"Not a *what*! A *who*, " responded Mona, in an equally loud voice. "The tape the driver is playing is of Omm Khalsum, one of the Arab world's most revered female singers."

"Is that right?" Jonathon said, unable to complement what he construed as meaningless tones and phrases.

"Pretty awful, isn't it?" Mona burst out laughing, intuiting what he was thinking.

"Now that you mention it, a resounding *yes!*" Jonathon replied, laughing. "But I don't want to offend you nor Ali."

"Mr. Miracle."

"Yes, Mona."

"There is no way you could ever offend me."

CHAPTER SIX

Atlanta

Ian McIntyre, Ph.D., was a formidable force in his field. A professor of physiology for 28 years at an Ivy League institution, he had made a "career shift", as he lightheartedly called it, to the speciality of epidemiology. He was first employed by the World Health Organization in Geneva, then later in Atlanta, where he was named director of the Crisis Intervention Section of the Centers for Disease Control. In his seventies now, he remained undaunted by age or illness, rising at dawn every morning for his stair-master exercises before his pre-breakfast walk. Never married, he was rumored to be a ladies' man, a fact he did not deny.

"So. I enjoy women, music, good food. Shouldn't every man?" he was apt to say when teased about his unabashed affection for female graduate students. To his credit, during all the years spent teaching, there was never a rumor of scandal or impropriety concerning his flirtatious activities. He was adored by students and faculty alike. True, his most loyal devotees were always female, but he offered, by way of explanation, that women were simply more demonstrative of their emotions while a man's first instinct when confronted with another male, was to become competitive and territorial.

Dr. McIntyre, however, was above such primitive squabbling. He was, above all, dedicated to science and to the sharing of knowledge, always *au courant* with the latest scientific information. He was fluent in five languages and a world traveler. Despite his many accomplishments there was a refreshing absence of arrogance about him, almost a childish energy which was noticeable in his encounters with others.

Consequently, to many people who did not know him well, he remained an enigma. Surely he had some faults, his critics would remark. A scandal involving a woman somewhere? But try as they might, his detractors reluctantly concluded that he was a man of genuine principle, somewhat obsessed with perfection, true, but nonetheless superior in most respects.

"Except singing," Jonathon told Mona, "and dancing," he added, as they disembarked from the flight from Cairo to Atlanta. He had persuaded Mona of the necessity of seeing his old friend and mentor before going on to Los Angeles. He told her it was a critical stop.

"Let's get a taxi right away and get going," he said as he hailed down a car. "The Centers for Disease Control," he directed the driver.

"Front entrance?"

"Yes. Thanks."

Turning to Mona, he continued his description of McIntyre. "What does he look like, you are probably thinking. Well, do you remember what Einstein looked like, with that wild hair? Sort of like that, although more like the composer Herbert von Karajan. But you wouldn't know him."

To Jonathon's surprise, Mona stated," Von Karajan is my mother's favorite conductor. I have seen his picture often on the tapes she has of his music."

"Pardon me. She's a connoisseur of music, then?"

"Well, I don't know about that," Mona added. "She's selective in her music although she claims to like it all, from heavy metal to Beethoven. But since I can remember she has been fascinated with von Karajan. Why do you keep asking me so many questions about her? Any why does this guy McIntyre have to get involved? Could he possible help her? I just want to get this over with and get to Los Angeles as soon as possible. I didn't count on this when I left Cairo."

"Hold on. Is your mother as outspoken as you are? Let me say something, Mona, about Dr. McIntyre. If your mother's life is at stake, and I told you no one there really knew what was wrong with her, McIntyre may possibly be able to figure it out, if it has something to do with a bacterial infection or a virus. Besides, we called Los Angeles from the plane, didn't we? Your mother is still on a respirator and her vital signs are not strong. The medical doctors there haven't a clue as to what is wrong with her or how to help her. Their only hypothesis, which now seems unlikely, is based on forensic speculation, that she overdosed on LSD. From your knowledge, is that possible?"

"My mother is an expert on LSD," Mona said defensively. "You really don't know much about her do you? Her doctoral dissertation was on the role of psychedelic drugs in the psychotherapy of intractably depressed patients. She was completing her research when my father left with us for Cairo. If she wanted to kill herself, she would have known exactly how much to take, so that it would have been over quickly. She would never have wanted to create a spectacle of herself with respirators, oxygen, paramedics, people staring at her, newspaper stories. She is a very private person. It's just totally opposite her nature. Never mind. When am I going to see this McIntyre person?" Mona said as the taxi came to a sudden stop. She had not been paying attention to the route.

"Did I hear a familiar name mentioned?" A smiling, dapper and completely disarming Dr. Ian McIntyre poked his white head into the open window of the taxi.

"Jonathon! What a pleasure. But you didn't have to come all the way here to Atlanta to tell me how well you performed on the Bateson case. I read all about it. You could have phone me! Of course, I am delighted to see you, welcome. And who is this beautiful young lady? May I have the pleasure . . ." he said as he adroitly opened the door for Mona and offered her his hand.

The irascible Dr. McIntyre had already stolen the show. "Mona, this is Dr. Ian McIntyre. We were just speaking about you, Ian," Jonathon remarked sheepishly.

"Well, hello. Welcome. Whatever Jonathon told you about me is all true. But what he didn't tell *me* is how beautiful Mona is. Please, by all means, come in."

Mona and Jonathon tried to match Dr. McIntyre's brisk sprint up the steps to his office. He skipped two steps at a time. Once inside, Jonathon took McIntrye aside at the coffee maker. He needed to quickly debrief him on the entire situation, from his arrival in Los Angeles, his quick trip to Cairo and what he found there-the petri dish and vial, particularly. He slipped those to McIntyre, who quickly handed them to his assistant. "For immediate analysis," he told her.

"It may not be anything," Jonathon mumbled defensively.

"You never know," McIntyre responded. When involved with anything to do with his work, he was dead serious. "We'll get the analysis soon enough. Always best to check everything out and assume nothing. It may *not* be anything, but then it could be everything you are looking for," he added as he and Jonathon rejoined Mona at the coffee table in the reception room of the Centers for Disease Control.

"What is *that* all about?" Mona asked, having noticed the seriousness of the interchange.

"I just wanted to give Dr. McIntyre an idea of your mother's case, from the time that I first saw her on the plane three days ago," Jonathon responded, feigning nonchalance.

"Don't worry about a thing, Mona," McIntyre immediately interjected. "Your mother is going to be all right," he presented his most reassuring smile.

"How do you know that?" Mona persisted, "you haven't even seen her."

"Mona, we're just . . ." Jonathon began, only to be quickly cut of by McIntrye.

"Yes. You're absolutely right, Mona. How would Jonathon here or myself or anyone not at the hospital on top of the situation know anything at all about the status of your mother? How do you know that I know anything about her? All I have is my intuition.

I gather as many facts as possible, then let it work. Of course, the objective scientific part is crucial. That is the area in which I was trained and which must be done perfectly, absolutely scrupulously, otherwise nothing good will ever come of any investigation. It must be done properly. But ultimately the end product will support, all things being equal, what your intuition has been telling you all along."

"Do you really believe that?" Mona asked. "I mean, the part about the intuition?"

"Absolutely I do. It's the key to everything. The driving force. You disagree?"

"Not. In fact, I agree 100%!" Mona asserted.

"Ah, nothing could please me more. I am a staunch believer in the power of the non-programmed mind. How about some coffee, tea, of a soft drink? Good. Excellent. We will all learn together in this time we have with each other. Your mother will recover and you will be with her soon. Don't ask me how I know this. In the meantime, I have already sent the contents of the petri dish and vial for thorough analysis."

"What petri dish?" Mona asked, confused.

"Uh. Mona," Jonathon began awkwardly. "I have to tell you something. I . . ."

McIntyre immediately interjected and rescued his friend and former student. "Mona, I have some crucial evidence to examine which may save your mother's life. Whether that evidence is in the form of a vial or a petri dish, or something else like a communique or a medical report, doesn't really matter. My job is to examine that evidence and then decide our next step."

"Oh. I understand," Mona said, completely mesmerized, much to Jonathon's astonishment and relief.

"I will inform you, of course, as soon as I can, about the connection, if any, between what is in the cultures we grow from the petri dish and any possible link to humans. Specifically, to you mother," he added, almost as an afterthought. "Leave all of that to me. I am very good at it. In the meantime, you will both spend the night here."

"What?" Mona shot up from her chair. "I can't do that! What if something happens to my mother? The whole reason I came here was to see her. I should be in Los Angeles right now, not here. I have to be back in Cairo in a few days. I can't waste time here!"

McIntyre stood up to face Mona. "A few moments ago, my assistant placed a call to the hospital in California where you mother is confined. The news is that she is in the best of hands. In fact, her physician is a former colleague of mine. Her breathing is being assisted by a respirator and she is being fed intravenously. She can safely remain in that situation for months. She people even stay on respirators for years. There isn't anything you or I can do for here except to explore the cause of her illness. That is the most important thing to accomplish right now. She would not even know you were there, Mona. Please. You must trust me. You will get there soon enough, when the time is right."

He paused, waiting for his words to take effect before continuing. "Let me explain something else. I have hypothesis, well, more like a hunch about this whole affair. That's where the intuition comes in. But we must explore everything to save your mother's life. You may have information which will lead me in the direction I need to go to find out her cure. Even hunches need some structure. Here is how I will proceed. I have some organic matter in a vial. I don't know what it is right now. It may or may not have anything to do with your mother's condition, but before we can definitely say that, we must identify what the organism is. That step will then engender a further hypothesis which hasn't even come to mind yet."

"What do you mean *identify?*" Mona asked.

"Good question, I like the student in you," McIntyre said immediately, maintaining eye contact with the girl at all times. He flashed her a gleaming smile. "I'll explain everything in exact detail when the time comes. When I have the answers. But first, please, let's have some refreshments."

In an instant as if on cue, the door swung open and two young men entered carrying trays of coffee and sandwiches.

"Thanks, gentlemen," McIntyre said, then turning to Mona, he added as they retreated quickly, "they are my research assistants. They have to do anything I tell them to do, including make sandwiches."

McIntyre glanced at Jonathon, who was squirming and who was hoping McIntyre wouldn't reveal that a few years ago, Jonathon was in just such a relationship with him.

But what he said instead was, "I don't know about both of you, but, as it is somewhere between dinner and bedtime, I need a little something to sustain me."

Completely disarmed now, Mona chose among the assortment. "I agree. I'm starved."

Jonathon marveled at how McIntyre was still able to turn a situation around to his benefit, to dispel an opponent's fears and anxiety, with such style and grace. Social amenities did not come naturally nor easily to Jonathon and he always noticed them in others. He privately admitted that in McIntyre he was observing one of the best social manipulators he had ever met.

"You are right. You have the absolute right to know what is going on here," McIntrye was saying to Mona between bites of his sandwich. "In fact, if I were you, I would demand it. First, we will try to replicate whatever is in the petri dish. Specifically, we want to try to grow another exactly like whatever *it* is. That will tell us whether it is still viable—-alive-or dormant. To accomplish that, we mix some of it with sand, add some sterile liquid, and place everything in another petri dish which will begin what we hope will become a successful culture. That will take about 6 to 8 hours. That is why you must stay overnight. Then we need a second test. Unfortunately, Mona, I hope you don't mind this part, but we have to inject some of what we produce in the petri dish into a few mice and wait just a few more hours to see what reaction they have, if any. That brings up to tomorrow, about noon. By then, I shall have more answers for you, and then you can leave to see your mother."

"Answers? About what?" Mona asked, still confused about the petri dish.

"What I mean is that I should know by tomorrow what has befallen you mother, if it is connected in some way with what is in the petri dish. We may know how to cure her. That I can promise you. That is why it is so important for you to remain here."

"Okay, I guess," Mona replied quietly. "I'm just not sure how you can know all of this from a petri dish. I don't see how the petri dish has anything to do with my mother. But I'm too tired to think about anymore," she continued and, turning to Jonathon, said, "are we going to find a hotel? I'm falling asleep."

"Hotel! Out of the question," McIntyre countered before Jonathon could respond. "You will stay at my home, it's just within walking distance from here. The walk is very pleasant. I insist."

Obediently, just like he used to do in medical school, Jonathon noted to himself, he and Mona unquestionably followed McIntrye's orders. He continued to talk amiably about research at the Center, walking arm and arm with Mona, while Jonathon stumbled along behind. McIntyre gave an extensive verbal history of the local faun and flora, beginning with the shrubs they were passing at the moment. A native of New York, he loved the natural environment after spending so many of his earlier years surrounded by skyscrapers with only Central Park as a reminder of nature. Now, devoid of city life, he clearly was enjoying himself.

"Of course," he added, "one is limited here to whatever cultural events are scheduled. In New York, I was spoiled with a multitude of choices-music, theater, dance, opera, symphony, unlimited restaurants. You name it, New York has it."

"I've never been there," Mona interjected somewhat self-consciously.

"No? What a shame, but easily fixable. I will show it to you, but after your mother recovers. You will both by my guests in my New York apartment. Promise? I still keep a large place on the

Upper East Side, and I will be delighted to show you everything there is to know about New York City."

Jonathon waited in vain to be included in the invitation but to no avail. He recalled his mentor's reputation as a lady's man. "Still at it," he said to himself as he continued to walk along behind the couple. "Certainly good at," he mumbled resentfully, despite the fact that he was at least thirty years Mona's senior, she was clearly enchanted by the old man.

At last they arrived at the McIntyre residence. It was a huge Tudor mansion.

"You can see where you will sleep, Mona," McIntyre stated, pointing to a third floor gable. "Right up there next to the stars."

Mona giggled, obviously enjoying being treated so specially. "Thanks, Dr. McIntyre," she said.

"Call me Ian."

Jonathon, accustomed now to being ignored, assumed that he would be sleeping in the basement quarters. He followed them into the exquisite house. Happily for Jonathon, the third floor contained a guest suite of four bedrooms. Mona's room overlooked the beautiful moonlit park. Jonathon's, the service entrance. But he wasn't complaining.

For a final goodnight, the trio met in the living room downstairs. Mona broached the inevitable personal questions to McIntrye: "Are you married?"

"No, no, afraid not, " he responded with the polished ease of years of answering the same question. "As a matter of fact, I never wanted to be, and I can't name one single happily married couple among all of my colleagues, students and ex-students. Like Jonathon here, who is divorced (I am right, old boy?) No. Physiology has taken over my entire life. Of course now, I look after the health of the world at the Centers for Disease Control. I am satisfied. Yes. And happy."

"I would never have thought," Mona stated hesitatingly," that a man could be happy not married, I mean, at least once!"

"Well," McIntyre was not taking the bait to expound more

about his personal life, "don't trouble yourself about the marital states of men, except those who show a marked interest in you. But enough of such serious talk! Goodnight, Jonathon. It's always a pleasure to see a former student. I take it the case in Jerusalem went well?"

Jonathon found it quite amazing that, outside of a brief introductory reference, McIntyre had not so much as alluded to the Bateson case. After all, it had been on the front pages of most of the international papers. Considering the fact that McIntyre had reneged on his commitment to accompany Jonathon at the Bateson hearing as an expert witness, and the fact that Jonathon was left to concoct a summation completely on his own, he felt that some explanation should be forthcoming. He could not, however, find it within himself to ask McIntrye for one.

Instead he said, "Oh. That. It went fine. Just fine."

"Great. No problem deciphering my notes on LSD I presume?"

"Piece of cake."

"I knew it would be, for you, Jonathon. I trained you. Of course, I want to hear all of the juicy details, but perhaps tomorrow. For now, have a good rest."

"Thank you so much for bringing me here, Jonathon," Mona remarked as they ascended the staircase together. "Dr. McIntyre is fascinating."

"Yes, he is. I told you. Well, goodnight."

Jonathon wondered, as he drifted into a deep, well-earned sleep, why he continued to have, after all these years, ambivalent feelings about his old mentor. Was it because he appeared so damned perfect? he thought to himself. Even in his mistakes, he manages to present them as advantages. Was it because McIntyre seemed so charismatically irresistible to everyone, even his enemies, while Jonathon paled beside him in terms of personal dynamic? Grudgingly, his brilliance and social skills *did* command respect. That could not be denied. Nor could one diminish his commitment to the welfare of his fellow man. He had traveled to Somalia in the early 1990's to help in the relief effort there (against the advice of the World Health Organization) and had helped to resettle thousands of children orphaned in the ethnic wars which engulfed Eastern Europe.

"It was one of the hardest things I have ever done," McIntyre had been quoted in a press conference, "to decide who to take and who to leave behind, to almost certain neglect, violence, starvation, and death. I chose the fittest because they would have the best chance of survival. It was an awful Darwinian ultimatum for me."

Later rumor had it that he had used a considerable amount of his own money to finance the project. "It was nothing, really," he had said at the time, brushing aside reports of his largesse. Privately he admitted that the obsequiousness of strangers toward him was beginning to irritate him. From that time on, he avoided all further public attention. He eschewed television appearances and shunned the press.

"What I crave more than anything else now," he mused, "is anonymity. What do I want with publicity? I want to live and to work alone and in peace."

"I know why he bothers me," Jonathon mumbled to himself as he drifted to sleep. "Because he is everything I have always wanted to be, and could have been, but somehow am not. I love that man but I hate him too. At the same time, I would defend him to the death." Sleep came as a welcome respite to Jonathon's conflicted thoughts.

The knocking on his door was abrupt and loud. "Just a minute," a sleepy Jonathon blurted out. "Who is it?"

"Mona. Do you know where Ian is?"

"Good morning to you, too. What time is it? How should I know where he is? Why didn't you wake me earlier?"

"I can't find Ian anywhere. I'm worried."

"Don't worry. What time is it?"

"It's almost 8 A.M."

"Okay, let me tell you something about *Ian*, " he said sarcastically, while putting on his robe and opening the door to his room. "As long as I have known him, he takes these early morning walks. That's *after* his exercises on those machines he keeps in his room, so that he stays in shape. Then he'll say he's 'earned his breakfast'. Don't look at me like that. I can't explain him. The man is almost 70 years old, but he's probably stronger than either you or I. He used to have a live-in housekeeper, Caitlin. Did you see her? She might be in the kitchen. I'll be right down."

"Is it okay if I go alone?"

"Sure. Have some coffee. I'll join you in a second."

During a wonderfully hot shower, Jonathon continued to rationalize his feelings about his former professor and mentor. It had not gone unnoticed by him that Mona was now using his first name. With a sigh, Jonathon decided to relinquish the jealousy he was feeling, despite his resentment of McIntyre's reputation of conquests of women, including Jonathon's own wife at one time. After all, nothing ever came of the innocent flirtations, that he could tell. McIntyre had never had the experience of a long-term relationship with a woman. And he did not have any children. Jonathon concluded that his behavior was a highly contrived form of entertainment for him and that he was incapable of the far more difficult undertaking of sustaining a marriage.

True, Jonathon's own marriage had ended in divorce, but it did last 10 years. He *did* make the commitment. "That took resiliency and determination", he said to himself as he dressed. Feeling enormously refreshed and fortified, he went down the staircase and opened the door to the breakfast room.

"Caitlin!" he literally shouted when he saw the short, shout, graying housekeeper, at the stove, turning pancakes.

"Well, well! If it isn't Dr. Miracle! Why you haven't changed a bit since medical school ! How are you? Are you remarried? Do you ever see that former wife of yours? Lovely girl, she was."

"Wait a minute, Caitlin," Jonathon chided, "I am *not* Dr. Miracle. I quite medical school, remember? I'm an attorney. And what's more . . ."

"And a fine one, I'd bet my last dollar on it!"

"Oh, Caitlin, it's so good to see you after all these years.

You look the same, not a day older. Has Dr. McIntyre been keeping you busy with his endless guests?"

"None of them as nice as you! But where did you find this beautiful girl! She says she lives in Cairo!"

There was a loud slamming of the door. "Ah! Good morning everybody!" Dr. McIntyre emerged from the garden.

"Good morning! I see Caitlin is still around," Jonathon teased.

"And thank God for that. What would I ever do without her? Yes, still with me, after all these years. Here, have some cheese with those croissants, the best you'll find this side of the Seine. I bought them for you this morning, while you two were submerged in slumber."

"Oh, here we go again," Jonathon smiled, "indolence, indolence, indolence."

Mona spoke up suddenly, "What a wonder gesture! I love croissants. Imagine, waking up before all of us, braving the morning chill, just to buy these. Thank you so much."

Jonathon could not help himself. He added, "Why, I'll bet you even cured that steel-cut orange marmalade over there, next to the cheese you probably aged yourself too!"

Laughs engulfed the kitchen as plates and coffee cups were filled. "I'm anxious, however, for a report on the petri dish," Jonathon whispered.

As if galvanized by Jonathon, Mona's attitude changed into strict seriousness. She resembled, to Jonathon now as he watched her, the stubborn young woman he met in the courtyard in Maadi.

"That's right. What did you find, Dr. McIntyre?" she said.

"Okay, we'll have a working breakfast. Fine with me. The petri dish in question has grown a particularly pernicious strain of Clostridium botulinum."

"Of WHAT?" Mona blurted out.

"Costridium botulinum, " he repeated. "You might recognize it as botulism. Ever hear of it?"

"Well, no, " Mona said quickly, then added, "Wait! I remember reading about an entire family of seven people in the United States who died after eating canned spaghetti sauce. It was even in the papers in Cairo. I think I remember the name botulism was somehow involved with it."

"Good memory, " McIntyre added. "That was the Murphy case. Yes. Upon autopsy, C. botulinum, the chemical name for the bacteria which causes botulism, was isolated in the livers of the victims."

"How awful," Mona recoiled in horror, her hand to her mouth.

"It's more awful than you think, " McIntyre continued. "Botulism is the cockroach of bacteria. It is the most deadly bacteria known to man, affecting its victims through a progressive paralysis. When it reaches the lungs, breathing stops. Death quickly follows. Botulism is six million times more poisonous than rattlesnake venom."

"Good God, Ian, " Jonathon commented, "how can people avoid ingesting it? How do you recognize it?"

"When people did more canning of their own food, we used to see a lot more botulism. You can tell it's inside the can when they bulge. And if the contents are not subjected to much heating before being eaten, the toxin immediately begins to destroy nerve endings. That means that neurotransmitters can't function, which in turn means that muscles don't get messages. Eventually they get completely blocked. People usually die of suffocation after the chest muscles become paralyzed. The survivors are lucky enough to have been put on a respirator, which breathes for them until their bodies can make new nerve endings. Are you following me?"

"Yes. I think so, " Mona replied. "But how was the toxin discovered?"

"A professor from the University of Wisconsin, named Schantz, isolated the toxin about 50 years ago. It was being studied as part of the U.S. biological warfare research program. But I would imagine it has been around since the earth was created."

"You mean the United States was planning to use it as a weapon against people?"

"Well, not exactly," McIntyre continued. "The CIA was

concerned about *other* countries using if first, on *our* troops. You know, in the '50's, there was a lot of experimentation going on, with the goal of biochemically destroying enemies. Or perhaps altering their personalities."

Jonathon spoke up, "That was the CIA's MK-ULTRA program, where LSD was given to unsuspecting American citizens."

"A perfect example of a secret agent of war," McIntyre expanded after Jonathon's input. "Whereas botulin loses its potency when it is exposed to air, LSD could be added to food or drink without any deterioration. Nor is it detectable. But botulin could still be used in an aerosol, for example, and remain lethal. During the Gulf War, if you recall, the U.S. Army was actually stockpiling the toxin. If it were ever to be used against our men, hopefully there would be antiserum developed and mass immunization could be begun. But there are other, more productive, more humanitarian uses for the deadly poison. For all sorts of dystonias-excuse me, Mona, for lapsing into scientific jargon-or movement disorders caused by too many transmitter receptors. The delicate injection of botulism into those areas would immobilize some of the nerve endings involved. The patient would then be free of dystonia-like symptoms, at least until he grew new nerve endings."

"What sorts of disorders could botulism help?" Mona asked.

"Well, so far, strabismus, and something called blepharospasm. Also cerebral palsy and multiple sclerosis. Fascinating, isn't it?"

McIntyre continued, "Getting back to botulism intoxication, however, if it is recognized early, the patient can be put on a respirator. Then about five weeks later, after the intoxication has run its course, he or she would awaken from the paralysis, perfectly normal in all respects. The problem, as you probably have already surmised, is that medical personnel might not recognize botulism as the source of the person's *dis-ease*. And, if unrecognized, botulism kills. In your mother's case, if we were to suppose that she were infected with it (and don't panic as I say this), whoever made the decision to put her on a respirator, in effect, saved her life."

Jonathon felt awash in pride. McIntyre had acknowledged his

competence, since it was he that had insisted that Sylvia be placed
on a respirator, when he saw her in the emergency room in Los
Angeles. True, he had not identified botulism, but he had saved
her life. And McIntyre recognized it.

"But before I continue, to put your mind at ease, Mona, I
took the liberty of telephoning St. John's Hospital in Santa Monica
early this morning. I ordered the antidote for botulism to be
administered to her as soon as it gets there. Do not worry. I don't
want you to fret while you are listening to this lecture."

Mona, spellbound, said, "But how can you be so sure that my
mother had botulism? How can you be so sure that your antidote
won't harm her!?

"Listen to me," McIntyre stared directly into Mona's eyes. "In
my capacity as head of epidemiological research here at the Centers
for Disease Control, I am one of the first to know of any outbreaks
of unusual bacterial proliferations anywhere in the world. I want
you to know that the week that your mother was in Cairo, I learned
that 25 Egyptians had died from a hybrid variety of C. Botulinum,
which, if I may add, even in its most common form is *rarely* found
in the Middle East. Corrections, it has *never* been recorded as the
cause of death of anyone in that part of the world!"

"It's not endemic in the Middle East, then?" Jonathon offered,
thinking aloud. "Then, that would mean . . ."

"Exactly. You have retained that medical investigative instinct
I encouraged in you, Jonathon. Wonderful. If a bacterium is not
endemic to a region, than means that someone or something had
brought it in or produced it. As a matter of fact, what makes *your*
vial so interesting is that it meshes with the current work I am
doing right now. When you asked me to testify at your case in
Jerusalem, although I was more than happy to do so, unfortunately
that week, myself and my colleagues here, received word of those
25 death in Egypt. This was the first known recorded incidence of
botulism poisoning in Egypt, or in the Middle East, for that matter,
ever. Can you understand the importance of the occurrence in
the history of epidemiology? We were put on a 24 hour alert.

We traded hypotheses. We brainstormed. One of our thoughts was that a terrorist had implanted the deadly bacterium into the dinner ingredients at a restaurant where the victims had all eaten together. Given all I have told you, Jonathon, do you now understand why I was unable to be at your side in Jerusalem, or even to tell you why?"

"Besides, " McIntyre continued, "in my opinion, and I mean this as a compliment of course, the outcome there was a foregone conclusion. I knew the Bateson boy would be freed. And I did send you more than the notes you would need to make a respectable presentation. All you really had to do was to read them, apply the logic, and the prosecution would have had no counterattack whatsoever, at least scientifically. My argument, as usual, was foolproof."

"But," McIntyre went on unabated, "I am getting sidetracked. Yesterday, Mona, you asked me how I would know if the bacteria we grew in the petri dish Jonathon gave me would be the lethal variety we were suspecting in your mother's case. That was the most interesting and important part of your visit here. We did not yet have a pristine sample of the new hybrid C. botulinum-which was the offender bacteria in Egypt. You, unwittingly, provided me with a remarkable service, also to the future safety of humanity, by bringing that vial here, although you did it for other reasons. Anyway, to go on. I hope you aren't getting faint-hearted. We injected a serum procured from that petri dish into some mice last night, after you had both gone to sleep."

"I told you that the only way to positively detect C. botulinum is through the intraperitoneal inoculation of mice. I thought we would not see a reaction until this afternoon. But, and this is a sign of the virulent strength of this bacteria's toxicity, we began observing positive signs within only a few hours."

"What do you mean, positive signs?" asked Mona, now enraptured by the story.

"Positive in the sense of serving science, but not for the mice, I'm afraid!" McIntyre joked. "We look for certain reactions, which always occur sequentially in the animals. First, ruffled fur. Then, labored breathing. Then weakness of their limbs. Finally, unfortunately, respiratory failure leading to a swift death."

"Oh, how awful, " Mona exclaimed. "But where did the botulism sample come from, I mean originally?"

"Clostridium botulinum has lived in the soil and in ocean sediment for millennium. It's found in the intestinal contents of birds and mammals. Its spores can be dust-borne, which is one way it contaminates food. It is also anaerobic. That means it can thrive in an oxygen-free environment. It cannot, however, compete with other bacteria which are killed by heating. The trick is, C. botulinum is resistant to heat, so long as it doesn't go above a very high temperature, where it will perish. So if the heat is not high enough, all the other surrounding bacteria will be destroyed thermally, except C. botulinum. It will then thrive! It is then very difficult to exterminate. More often it becomes dormant, but easily revived under warm conditions, even years later. The point is, that unless the temperature gets to be extremely high, it will not touch this bacteria."

"Isn't there *anything* which can hurt it?" Mona continued.

"You mean, besides intense heating?" McIntyre answered. "Well, yes, actually, there is. Ascorbic acid. Or as you would know it, Vitamin C-is lethal to botulism spores. If heating is used as the method of destruction, it must be sustained for at least 15 minutes, because the spores don't die before then."

"Insufficient cooking of food which might have the bacteria in it can be deadly."

"Exactly."

"Well," Mona retorted, "what could my mother have eaten which might have had botulin in it? She was with us when she was in Egypt, the entire time."

"Try to look at it this way," McIntyre continued. "Botulin can exist in *any* oily dense medium which has not been heated to the boiling point and remained there for 15 minutes. Do you recall anything she might have eaten which might have been like that?"

Mona was silent for a long time before responding. "She had dinner with us only three times. The last time was at an open air restaurant in the Moqqattan Hills near the Citadel. The only possible thing we ate which was not cooked for hours was the hummus. It's a bean dip."

"A bean dip?" McIntyre perked up. "Perfect! Beans are protein, a nurturing environment for the bacteria. Was the dish also mixed with any oil?"

"Yes," Mona replied. "That's how it's made. Olive oil. But something is very wrong with what you're thinking."

"What's that?"

"Not only did my mother eat the bean dip, but so did my brother Tarif and so did I. We didn't become sick at all."

"Hmmm. That's a thought. But maybe not. We have to go through the sequence of events carefully, over and over again. As for me, I am certain that we have found the culprit."

"What's the next step, then?" asked Mona.

"Sending the antidote to California," McIntyre said quickly. "But that's already been done."

"How did you get an antidote?" Mona persisted.

"Mona, " McIntyre joked, "have you ever considered taking a course in biochemistry or physiology? I'll bet you'd really like it. But to answer your question, we normally inject a small amount of the toxin into horses, whose blood develops antibodies to it. Antibodies are what we are looking for and what we take back from the horse in the form of serum. Recently, a synthetically-produced drug called '3-4 diaminopyridine' has been developed. In fact, as a chemically-produced antidote, it brings remarkable improvement within only a few days."

"Is that what you sent my mother?"

"Yes. That is exactly what she is receiving as we speak. I can see that you love her very much," McIntyre smiled. Mona looked away, embarrassed.

"Dr. McIntyre?" Caitlin appeared in the doorway.

"Yes!"

"The gentlemen from the government who phoned this morning have arrived."

"Thank you, Caitlin. Mona, Jonathon, I have some bad news. Not about your mother, Mona, but about this entire case. It seems that, well, I am not as good at criminal theories as I am at biological ones, so perhaps we should all go to the library and let my guest Lieutenant Brady explain."

"Criminal theory?" Mona exclaimed.

"Don't worry, my dear. They want us to verify their theories, that's all. They piece together ideas, make up protocols, all of that, " McIntyre answered ad Jonathon rose to the occasion by shifting to his hyper-alert mode. This was *his* territory.

"Who does Lt. Brady work for, Ian?" Jonathon quickly asked as they walked to the library.

"The Central Intelligence Agency."

"I should have known, " Jonathon said. "How did *they* get involved?"

"Okay, I'll quickly go through the sequence. Later I'll give you more detail. As I told you before, I have been deeply involved in the botulism poisoning case in Egypt. The importance of it was that no outbreak of botulism had ever occurred there. We always pay attention to new sites of a virus or bacteria. I have been keeping meticulous notes, which are available to any government agency which wishes to see them. Of course, when we discovered the nature of the bacteria you brought me in that petri dish, I added that information to my computer log. I was somewhat surprised to hear from the CIA within an hour of entering the data. It's both reassuring and disconcerting, I would say. In any event, let's not keep Lt. Brady waiting."

"Mona?" McIntyre said pointedly.

"Jonathon is the only person the Lieutenant needs to speak with at this point. Please don't take offense. You'll be next, I assure you. Those CIA agents are incredibly boring, you know. Anyway, how about another cup of coffee with me? And Caitlin has been dying to find out about Cairo. Do you resemble your mother?"

While Mona and Dr. McIntyre returned to the kitchen, Jonathon entered the library, expecting to find a clone of PSYCOPS. He was pleasantly surprised to find Lt. Brady to be a mature, seasoned federal agent with good manners, a sense of humor, and a sharp intellect. Somewhat conservative and a little racist, Jonathon thought later, but then again, he told himself, liberals don't make good career CIA people.

"Miracle. Bob Brady," the Lieutenant shook Jonathon's hand firmly and smiled reassuringly.

"Just a few questions, Jonathon. You don't mind my calling you Jonathon, do you? Dr. McIntyre probably told you why I'm here. We routinely monitor his databases in order to keep abreast of his monthly briefings to us. We do that just in case something comes up in the interim. That's how we discovered the recent recurrence of polio and tuberculosis way in advance of any other country. Of course, we only pass along that sort of information because we aren't really in the health business."

"You are now," Jonathon quipped.

"Right. I'm sure you have some idea of our cooperation with McIntyre."

"Yeah, I do."

"Uh-huh. Funny, I specifically told him not to mention it."

Jonathon and Bob Brady enjoyed a healthy laugh together.

"I'll get to the point, Jonathon. Our motive is not exactly identical to McIntyre's. We're not in the health business, as I said. He's interested in the documentation and prevention of epidemics and accidents. Our aim is to halt the advancement of biological warfare research and development. R & D in countries other than our own, of course."

"Come one, you know that's impossible," Jonathon retorted. "China has been experimenting with biochemicals for several decades now."

"True. But what's okay for China is *not* okay, from our point of view, for Iraq or for Iran. Get the picture?"

"Sure," Jonathan replied. "Crystal clear."

"China nudges along with its economic and social ascendancy efforts. But Iraq and Iran are far more volatile. And unstable. That means unpredictability, militarily-speaking. Therefore, read in dangerous and potentially uncontrollable. We can't let things get out of hand. We cannot, under these circumstances, allow unrestricted experimentation with psychologically of biochemically-acting drugs in unstable Middle Eastern countries. The purpose of such experimentation is to either destroy or to control people. Middle Eastern countries, among others in the Third World, are not what you can call . . ."

"Mature enough politically to handle grotesque forms of human torture?"

"Exactly right, Miracle. They don't see the big historical picture and probably never will. Their minds are entombed in ancient family and religious feuds: a little land here, a little land there. The settling of old scores, the living in the past. Whenever a conflict in the present crops up, all those centuries of old hostilities are lumped on top of it. This makes it not one isolated conflict, but an insurmountable volcano of collective, seething emotion with very little logic mixed in."

"Why should that be so different from the recent struggles of European countries trying to unite under the common market?" Jonathon began enjoying himself now, finding Brady interesting as the interchange of their ideas and expressed biases took on a more intellectual direction.

"True. Good point. Yes, there was a lot of bickering about the Maastricht Treaty. Yes, Germany and France started getting xenophobic again in their own inimitable ways. But in the long term, and that's really the point, isn't it, the long term-Miracle, the European community can perceive that the advantage of economic and political cooperation outweighs such temporary anachronistic temper tantrums. But no, not the Middle East. There, the *present* means *forever.*"

"You mean the *present* means the *past*." Jonathon and Brady had a good laugh.

"But what about Palestine," Jonathon continued.

"What about it? It's not *my* specialty, but just from personal observations, there are only two interesting items between Israel and Palestine. All that religious posturing about Eretz Israel on the one hand, and that "pushing Israel into the sea" on the other, is a bunch of crap. Unfortunately, that's all the world sees. That's all that the press reports. The real issue, which made the tide turn in favor of the creation of an independent Palestinian state, was pure economics."

"So you're a Marxist, eh?" Jonathon laughed in spite of himself.

"Call it what you will," Brady was not amused. "I'm not a political genius. But if you have followed the news and maybe even perused the Internet occasionally, you would have concluded that when the economy of Israel was in tatters, so was that of the United States. I'm speaking historically, now. At the same time, what always happened? We turned inward, focusing on our own domestic problems and economy. Translated into foreign policy, that meant less money for other so-called struggling countries and worthy causes, like national determination. Therefore, the nearly bankrupt Israel had to face its Achilles Heel. Finally."

"Which was?"

"Integration into the greater Arab region, and not particularly on its own terms, either. It's simply and obviously outnumbered."

"And the second part of your theory?"

"Oh, yeah. That. Well, that's the touch-feely part. I sort of think of the Palestinians becoming the torch-bearers and the nemesis, sort of, of the Arab world."

"Can you explain?"

"Sure. When you have a people facing extinction, annihilation and genocide, and then suddenly given them their freedom and dignity back, in the form of a national identity and a *land* (or at least part of it), they have a unique historical opportunity to do what amounts to re-inventing themselves collectively as a people, as a distinctive social personality. Look at them as hybrids, in the best sense of the word. That is, taking the most progressive elements of their history and culture and fusing them with the economic opportunities of the present and future."

"But isn't that what the Jews attempted to do in 1948?" Jonathon wondered.

"Yes and no. Yes, because they had that born-again fervor, an indispensable quality. No, because they lured thousands upon thousands of people from everywhere in the world, including Russia and the Arab countries, and had them immigrate. They probably would have been better staying where they were. Why? Because they did not share that Ubermensch philosophy of the European Jew."

"Wow! But I though that Israel's founders wanted every Jew in the world-rich or poor-educated or not, to join in its resurgence."

Brady yawned. "That's ideology, not economics. If you look at what that policy engendered, you will see an influx over the years of masses of unskilled and backward people. All they were offered was promises and handouts-paid for, by the way, by American dollars. They created a welfare state supported by the United States. Where were the jobs? Where were the markets? The one obvious market glaring Israel right in the face is the Arab world. But they can't have their cake and eat it, too, if you know what I mean. They can't confiscate Palestinian land under the guise of some ancient book which only they believe in, and offend in the process the immense Arab culture, as well as a good many Western countries, and then expect to do business with the same people!"

"Mind if I get us some coffee?" Jonathon interjected, returning quickly with 2 steaming cups. "I hope you like it black."

"No problem. See, there are many part of Israel today, usually the Sephardic parts, that are slums. Israel can't expect American money to remake their country for them and to finance their armies against an aloof Arab world, which, by the way, is becoming more interesting to us as economic partners than as political enemies. It was, from the beginning, a schizophrenic political philosophy. The U.S. has its own homeless and unemployment problems. It finally dawned on Israel that it needed to bite the bullet of reality. It was going to have to deal with its own problems. It no longer had the luxury of having someone else (the U.S.) paying its bills, while it plays games with the Palestinians. Israel made itself into a welfare state with many of its people living on the dole while the government kept pouring money into military campaigns."

"Can I interject?" Jonathon began, "In a way, isn't it like the Israelis having to face what the U.S. did after Bush lost to Clinton? I mean the country was neglected domestically because of the attention focused on foreign affairs during the Bush era."

"Yeah," Brady agreed. "Clinton's America developed its work force, its infrastructure, its educational systems and paid less attention to foreign intrigues of domination and confrontations and control over other people and their land. Israel had to do that, too. Forever battling Palestinians and the Arab culture in general, was going to be a no-win situation. They finally realized it. They had to regard their enemies as equal partners in the overall prosperity of the region and drop their self-imposed role of bully, because the whole world realized it anyway.

"Listen, Brady," Jonathon chided, "how many people in your office are aware of your political opinions?"

"They're no secret. Whether you're pro-Israeli or pro-Palestinian, these days the issue is really passe, you know. We want stability there. There's a lot of money that can be made, that's as crass and frank an answer as I can give you. So the Israelis have to grow up. So what? I've paid my dues, so I can speak my mind. I stay within reasonable bounds. Israel has got to get itself off the Arab embargo, in deed as well as in word, in order to do business with its neighbors. That was not going to happen if a Palestinian state was not going to happen. That brings us up to date. Our fledgling Palestinian state and the emergence of a true middle class in the Middle East. That brings with it instability and uncertainty, also aspirations, plans, determination."

"Then drugs, anxiety, psychotherapy, upward mobility," Jonathon inserted.

"That too. But let's get to the present topic here. We've been watching Dr. Huzam, Mona's father and Sylvia Grieg's former husband, for a long time. For one thing, he has quite a few unnumbered bank accounts in Switzerland and in Liechtenstein. For another, he takes monthly trips to Iraq from Egypt. Our surveillance in Iraq has uncovered some activity in chemical research. We aren't presuming that Huzam's interest is humanitarian, judging from his background. Since the ban on the transportation of nuclear components to Iraq, it has turned to more traditional yet more innovative means of chemical warfare."

"Nerve gas? Neurobiochemical agents?" Jonathon asked.

"Right. It's been clear to us for some time that Huzam has been involved with Iraq in the production of C. botulinum, one of the deadliest poisons man has ever known. Coincidentally, there has recently occurred isolated outbreaks of botulism in areas of the world where it has never been recorded before."

"Like the Middle East," Jonathon added. "McIntyre told us. Do you have enough on Huzam to put him away?"

"We think so, particularly now with the 12 Egyptians who died of botulism poisoning a few weeks ago. We can trace those deaths back to Huzam fairly easily. The Egyptian government is also very interested in the case and is cooperating with us. We have a good case against him, in fact, provided that you don't decide to become his attorney, Miracle."

"You're joking. You must know that I'm his ex-wife's attorney. I'm convinced right now that she had nothing to do with his illegal activities with botulism, not with any plot to ship LSD from the Middle East to this country or anywhere else, despite the fact that she knows so much about it."

"I'm sure you'll be relieved," Brady said, "that the CIA shares your view regarding Sylvia Grieg. But we want her to help us get Huzam. Our interest is in cutting his connection to Iraq, where he is selling his knowledge and expertise about botulism and its effects on the human body for profit. I think of him as a neurologic mercenary."

"How do I fit into all of this?"

"I knew you'd be asking that sooner or later. Our plan is for Sylvia to return with you to Cairo, identify Huzam, and provide testimony against him. The Egyptian government will provide backup. What does she get? Her son Tarif back."

"Did I hear that we were going back to Cairo?"

"Sorry, pal. Yes. As soon as Sylvia can make the trip. Huzam is due back in Cairo in 3 days. The one question I have in my mind is how cooperative the daughter Mona will be. We can't, of course, have Huzam tipped off."

"That I can't answer, Brady. In my opinion, she is an intelligent and strong-willed young woman. But she loves both her mother and father. Cooperating with your agency in the apprehension of her own father might be a very difficult thing for her to do. I know you're going to try, though. Good luck. She's probably waiting to talk to you right now."

Jonathon Miracle must have looked a little stunned when he left the library, because Mona blurted out, "Is everything all right? What's wrong?"

"What?" Jonathon responded. "Everything's fine. Brady is okay. Just so you know. He wants to speak to you now."

"Are you sure? Well, okay." Mona quietly opened the library door.

Jonathon slumped in a chair beside McIntyre who said, "I have no doubt that she's do it."

"Yeah, I think so too. But at what personal cost to her? An can she be trusted in the end?"

"Don't worry about it, " McIntyre countered. "Let her intelligence and her heart guide her. When she sees her mother on a respiratory, she'll know what to do. Brady is giving her an idea of her father's illegal activities. That's going to be difficult for her to come to terms with. Her feelings will be churning when she leaves him. Be careful with your comments. She's high-spirited. In fact, why don't you go for a walk?"

"Who will be here for her, then?"

"Caitlin. She's great with cocoa and chocolate chip cookies

after chicken soup, you know. Believe me, we've had some situations around here over the years where I've come to value her. She has that no-nonsense, down-to-earth, 'life is trouble' attitude, which is, oddly enough, comforting. Mona will face a revision of her private world and the people inside of it. That will be extremely difficult. But she has to do it."

"I can't wait to get out of here," Jonathon blurted out. "Any suggestions where to go?"

"Sure. How about catching an exhibit? That'll take your mind off things. Go see *Outsider Art* at one of the museums a few blocks from here. Let's go together. The walk will do us good physically and the art will do us good existentially."

"Since when have you been interested in art?" Jonathon asked.

CHAPTER SEVEN

Los Angeles

Mona had been quiet and introspective since leaving Atlanta. Jonathon thought it best not to disturb her with polite but idle conversation. So her buried himself instead in one of his forensic novels. Yesterday, Mona did not speak about her conversation with Brady, who simply nodded his head in affirmation when they both left the house together. Dr. McIntyre and Jonathon were in excellent spirits after having a spirited discussion of the meaning of art in modern society. They had gone out for dinner, packed and left very early for the airport.

She slept most of the route and missed the dramatic approach to the Los Angeles basin, the tangle of freeways and cars, the mountains and the ocean, an ominous menace in the background. Still undecided as to whether she was going to accompany him back to Cairo, he prepared himself mentally to confront Sylvia Grieg.

"Do you mind if I drive? It would make me feel better, " Mona asked straightaway as Jonathon unlocked the door to his Ford Mustang convertible.

"No. Go ahead. Top up, or down?"

"Down."

"Sure. Do you mind some advice about driving in L.A.?" Jonathon ventured without waiting for an answer. "Los Angeles has more policemen per square mile than any other American city. They are involved for the most part in trapping drivers who are going somewhat over the speed limit on the massive freeway systems, or not wearing their seat belts, or simply jaywalking. It's been this way since the State of California began the practice of issuing I.O.U.'s to its employees instead of paychecks, sometimes shortly after Christmas, because it traditionally runs out of money around the end of the year. So, bilking citizens out of their money is considered fair game. The people are on the highways trying to make it to work on time. So they speed a little? But about now is the time when the public becomes fodder for the coffers of the L.A.P.D. Just so you know to be careful about speeding."

"I get it, I get it," Mona remarked impatiently, then sped off onto the road leading to Imperial Highway from the airport. Jonathon decided to play some quiet Bach cello suites on the CD player in the hope that it would have a calming effect on her. She seemed unusually intense and quiet after the encounter with Lieutenant Brady. She didn't seem to be aware of her own tension. Jonathon, on the other hand, was unusually apprehensive about the imminent meeting of mother and daughter, given the circumstances.

Mona's words about Sylvia still rang in his ears, "My mother is dead," she had shouted. Clearly she had put a large part of the blame for her parent's divorce on her mother. He wondered if, because of her present mood, he should warn the personnel at the hospital, which they were fast approaching, of a possible volatile scene between them. After all, Mona had been through a lot the past few days, and seemed to be seething with emotion. In fact it just might be that what he was witnessing now was an expression of her rage, as she floored the Mustang, soaring past squad cars and other vehicles at 75 miles per hour. Fortunately they did not follow because he didn't even check if she had a driver's license with her.

He felt that further lectures to her would go unnoticed and would just irritate her more, so he sulked in silence, listening to Yo-Yo-Ma's meticulous cello. Her driving was well timed, coming to a stop at the hospital exactly when the CD ended. They were in Santa Monica.

"This has got to be awfully hard on you," Jonathon said more to himself than to Mona as they reached the Internal Medicine Unit where Sylvia had been transferred. "I called the hospital while you were asleep on the plane. She is awake now and probably will be able to recognize and speak to you," he offered gently.

Mona didn't respond at all, ignoring him in fact, and continued to look forward as the elevator door opened and they stepped forward into the hallway of 3 West, heading straight for the Nurses' Station. Jonathon trailed behind her, feeling awkward, trying to think of something to say to make the meeting more successful. He was mentally prepared for the worst: tears, sobbing, possibly rage, accusations, even hair-pulling. As they were let through the door to Sylvia's room, Jonathon would never forget one of the strangest sights he would ever see.

"No. It's *you!*" a vibrant Sylvia Grieg, sitting up in bed, exclaimed as Mona virtually flung herself into bed with her. Hugging each other, Mona convulsed in laughter. Tears streamed down Sylvia's face as well as Mona's, but they were tears of happiness, not anger. They embraced silently for a long time. Jonathon stood silently by shuffling his feet.

"Mom! Do you know Jonathon Miracle?"

"Should I?"

"He's your attorney?"

"In that case, how are you, Jonathon Miracle."

The nurses thought the joke was on Jonathon too, as everyone seemed to be enjoying themselves, except him. He felt intensely uncomfortable. He felt colossally foolish. Sylvia had practically died, Jonathon had bought a ticket with his own money for her daughter to travel from Cairo to Los Angeles via Atlanta. Everyone believed Sylvia was on her deathbed.

He felt his altruism had tricked him again. He had found a noble gesture irresistible, then resented it later when he felt used by a person or a group who had their own way of thinking.

"Don't take it so seriously," Sylvia chastised him.

"Yeah, Jonathon! Lighten up," Mona chimed in.

"I have no idea what you mean," he said. "I have devoted a

great deal of time and money to try to be of some help, for no other reason than that I believed an injustice might have been done to an innocent person."

"Who?" Mona asked.

"Never mind," he retorted.

"Please. Who?"

"Your mother, who else?" Shifting his gaze to Sylvia, he continued, "When you were taken off that plane at death's door and brought to this hospital, maybe you'd like to know that I was the one who made sure you were put on a respirator as soon as possible. That probably saved you life, in case you don't realize it. Then the prosecutor, on very little evidence, was going to charge you with an international drug conspiracy, for which you would have been sentenced to thirty years to life with no possibility for parole."

"You really saved me from all of that?" Sylvia rebounded, immediately becoming serious.

"Yes."

"You either saved me or damned me, I'm not sure yet," she added.

"I say that I saved you."

"In that case, thank you, " she said flatly. "Now what do we do?"

Before Jonathon could answer, Mona burst forth with an itinerary which she had apparently already discussed with Lieutenant Brady. She seemed to have no thought for the implications for her father.

"First, we travel to Cairo."

"Again? When?" asked Sylvia.

"Tomorrow."

"Excellent," Sylvia added, excitedly. "Then?"

"Then," Mona continued slowly, at the airport, you and I will wait in the Four Star Lounge, and . . ."

"You're sure it's Four Star?" Sylvia joked.

"Mom, listen. When Dad arrives from Baghdad with Tarif,

the CIA will confront him, along with the Egyptian and Iraqi Secret Police. He'll be arrested, Tarif will be taken to us in the Lounge."

"Will you father be harmed in any way?" Sylvia asked placidly.

"The international press corps will be there," Mona said. "I made that a condition of our participation in this arrangement with Lieutenant Brady in Atlanta. The presence of the press and their follow-up should insure that Dad will not be mistreated in any way and that he will be given due process, " Mona repeated Brady's terminology almost verbatim.

"Where did you say you were, Atlanta?" Sylvia asked. "What in the world were you doing there?"

"Mom, there's this professor there, from the Centers for Disease Control. His name is McIntyre. He knows a lot of the things you do about neurochemicals. He's really cool."

"You don't mean Ian McIntyre, do you?" Sylvia asked, "He's my hero."

At last Jonathon had an opportunity to establish some rapport. "He was my professor and advisor when I was in medical school, " he interjected.

"But I though you were a lawyer," Sylvia asked, puzzled.

"Well, I am a lawyer, but I went to medical school for 2 years before opting for law school. How do you know him?"

"He's only the world's foremost authority on biochemical processes and has done the most research on LSD, in which I am very interested. I have always wanted to meet him."

"We are going to meet him," Mona burst out."He's invited all of us, including Tarif, to his home in Atlanta, to recuperate, after Cairo. Don't say No, Mon, please, wait 'till you meet him."

"I didn't say anything," Sylvia smiled at her daughter.

Jonathon, in his compulsion to do things correctly, could help himself from blurting out, as if he had anything to do with it, "Of course, we have to check with the medical staff here, to make sure it's safe for your mother to leave," he said in a strange voice he did not recognize as his own. And why was he talking to Mona instead of to Sylvia?

"Mr. Miracle, " Sylvia looked at him straight in his eyes, "I am leaving here tomorrow on a flight to Cairo. Mona will be with me. I assume you will also, my self-appointed attorney, whom I accept. I can assure you that the medical staff here will not pose a problem. And you can tell your CIA friend Brady that I will more than cooperate with him."

Jonathan never felt so miserable in his life. In his vain attempts to establish control in the situation, he had completely misread the relationship between Sylvia and Mona. Now his place seemed to have been relegated to a mere accompaniment to the main drama or perhaps, just a buffoon. He sensed the old feelings of resentment building, those spikes of cold emotion which seemed to pierce him in the company of especially confident women, those who knew what to do in situations without asking a man. His unresolved struggle made him uncomfortable. Why, he thought, do I have this difficulty? Was it a power sense in him which, when thwarted, led to his emotional withdrawal? Why should it matter that Sylvia and Mona did not play out the roles he had envisioned for them as he was flying to Los Angeles? Hard as it was to face, Jonathon had to admit that it appeared to be a problem with control. He wanted to control *them*, not vice-versa.

Feeling distinctly uncomfortable, he excused himself for the evening. Sylvia and Mona hardly noticed. Mona had fallen asleep on the cot next to her mother, who appeared to be lost in reverie, oblivious to whether he was present or not. He made a mental note to be there to pick them up around 11 A.M. the next morning, then he slipped out of the room without looking back. He desperately needed to regain his emotional equilibrium. Or was it his identity? He felt he had to reestablish within himself his substance, his drive, his purpose. This state of estrangement and angst was not new to him. Whenever he felt engulfed in it he took an extremely long walk with no particular destination in mind. His legs would be aching and his chest heaving at the end, as if he had to wear his physical body out. That is what he was driven to do the evening before the Bateson trial, when he found the Via Dolorosa in Jerusalem.

On this occasion, Santa Monica beach would have to do. It was, after all, one of the most beautiful beaches in the world. While crossing Pacific Coast Highway he carefully pieced together in his mind the events of the last few weeks. He gingerly stepped onto the bikers' blacktopped path a few feet from the pounding surf. He allowed his thoughts to roam and immediately he was questioning his decision to defend Michael Bateson in the first place. That action, after all, had led to the domino effect of everything else he had experienced in the past 2 weeks. One not-too-carefully-considered decision. Why had he fallen so easily, he wondered, for the attraction of a new experience? Usually he spent at least a couple of days considering the advantages, disadvantages and merits of an appeal. Yes, intellectual challenge was important, but in the Bateson case there did not appear to be much of that.

It was an obvious subliminal attraction. He saw in Bateson a replica of his younger brother, whom he had similarly rescued a few years ago. It was a moment he would never be able to forget. For one, it was his first case. He had given up his marriage for a career in law and it was important for him to justify the expense and effort it had taken to get him to the point where he could function as a member of the bar. His devotion to his brother had overcome his dedication to his wife, and the trauma he caused her was a factor in his present feelings of guilt. True, he rationalized, the marriage had long before reached the stultifying point where it made no difference to either of them whether they ever saw each other again. Why bother to keep appearances, he thought? Why wait around for a spark to be re-ignited?

Mary Ann never understood, despite the dozen or so years they had been married, his inner drives and passions and contradictions. She only saw her own needs-a position in society, a title, money. How could she know that Jonathon would never forgive himself for abandoning his brother during the exciting early courtship period of their relationship and the grueling two years of medical school which followed their marriage? How could she know that he often awoke from dreams about his brother in prison which left him in a cold sweat? Even when he tried to explain, several times, she made it clear that such inner workings should not be shared, at least with her.

She had made it clear that in her view, her brother-in-law should experience the consequences of his choices, and that Jonathon would do well to allow that to happen. "That's how people *learn*," she used to say. "We should stay away. Why did he go to those rock concerts? What did he find so appealing in those people he hung around with? None of them were in school, none of them had jobs. He should have suspected that they were making money through drug trafficking or some other illegal activity. While I know you don't believe he ever had anything to do with the drug stuff, he was naive and worse, stubborn. Now he has to pay for it."

Mary Ann did not believe that anyone should be rescued from the consequences of their choices and could not understand why Jonathon felt so duty-bound to rescue his brother. It was a constant point of contention throughout their marriage. Jonathon was forced to comply with her views in the early years, just to keep harmony between them. He even envied her fortitude. Only later did he realize that what he originally construed as moral tenacity was merely pugnacious self-righteousness and well-disguised self-interest.

Since their divorce, she had married one of her former college boyfriends, continuing to lead a life identical to the one she wanted to share with him. "She merely substituted him for me," Jonathon thought out loud, as he dodged someone racing toward him on a mountain bike in the dark.

If the decision to follow his passion and loyalty toward his brother contributed to the dissolution of his marriage, he seemed to continually need to rehearse over and over again in his mind, his reasons for doing so. Even after his brother was free, he kept reliving his trauma. He sought out similar cases to defend, even those discarded by other attorneys, in order to justify to himself, his earlier actions. He desperately needed something more in his life now, than simply patching up the mistakes of others, via the courtroom. He wanted to believe that he had the power to rescue people from themselves, from those unfortunate situations into which they had fallen through their own unwitting actions, not because they were evil, but because they were stupid, inexperienced, idealistic, or immature. Why should those be reasons to spend the rest of your life behind bars?

He believed his brother had become involved in events and with people who could have destroyed him. There were thousands of other young people just like him: young, naive, confused, and passionate about life and truth. If they came from the upper classes in society, they were saved from themselves by their families and the money they had to hire expensive attorneys who would quietly take care of these youthful blunders. If not, which is more likely the case, they had their youth snatched away from them by the criminal justice system, forced to spend decades in prisons in small towns away from their families, from society, friends, education, anything positive which might uplift them, which might provide the impetus to re-evaluate their actions. They became bitter. Some of them never got away from the prison system. They became institutionalized, couldn't live on the outside anymore.

Rigid moralists would say "they had it coming", yet Jonathon knew better. He was revolted by such reductionistic and simplistic logic. He believed, he thought as he walked along in the dark on the beach, that life was an intricate mosaic which was always in flux. Where we find ourselves in that mosaic when we are born is sheer chance. To imagine that the solutions of a generation ago could be considered permanent, or that people were not changed by their environments, or by their physiologies, was insane. He passionately believed in the positive (or negative) effect of one personality on another. He believed in the strength of relationships to cure. That is why he chose to defend his brother and since then, hundreds like him, for little compensation relative to the work he put into their cases. He realized that the concept of the power of the mentor relationship, which he had experienced firsthand when he was under the tutelage of Ian McIntrye, could indeed create wonders, could turn lives and minds around, and he wanted to be the kind of person who could do that, who could be that, for others.

Yet, on this particularly cold night on the Pacific Coast Highway, he felt that he fell ridiculously short of his ideal. It was a dissonance he had felt since Mona and he had arrived in Atlanta which stuck to his thoughts now, depressing him and causing him to question everything that he had done in his life. The dysphoria was becoming acute.

He remembered how McIntyre had the uncanny talent of forcing people to face themselves. He had a bag of tricks to accomplish this. Sometimes Jonathon thought these efforts were intrusive, childish, and worthless. At other times he realized how powerful a few words can be. Now, as the ocean winds were whipping up, Jonathon felt vulnerable, cold, and intensely alone. Why did he feel so empty? Did he covet McIntyre's power over other people, his charisma, his magnetism, his charm? Perhaps he really hated him, but he dismissed that thought immediately, and turned eastward, walking to his home now, thinking that he had not make much progress on this lonely walk, in trying to confront himself and his uneasiness about Sylvia, Mona, and McIntyre. He was only scratching the surface, he concluded.

The next morning, the sun sparkled off the polish of the limo as it slowly rolled to a stop in front of St. John's Hospital. Sylvia and Mona walked quickly out of the hospital's front doors as if on cue. They looked radiant. "Good morning, Jonathon!" they said together, their smiles and energy infectious. He could not help but be affected.

"How's the patient this morning?" he tentatively offered.

"Which one?" Mona inserted. They all laughed and Sylvia added, "I'm actually very well now," a serious look transforming her face as she seated herself beside Jonathon in the back of the car.

"Being a patient was quite an experience. I did some reading about botulism poisoning this morning. Did you know that I was conscious during the entire ordeal, even on the plane?"

"You're kidding!" Jonathon remarked, thinking that if that were the case, she had been aware of the entire situation prefacing the drama they were now concluding.

"No, I'm not. Botulism produces paralysis in every system in the body, except one's consciousness. I heard every noise, every word, every action, when I was not asleep."

"I'll bet there are some people who would be rather embarrassed to know that now," Mona added.

"Could be. But the antidote came just in time to save me from some absurd experiments the local medical people there were contemplating, in conjunction with the L.A.P.D."

"What do you mean?" Jonathon asked, puzzled.

"Like scheduling me for a magnetic resonance imaging scan after infusing me with LSD."

"What!"

"Yes. I heard them discussing it. They wanted to see if my brain was turned on when they placed what was supposed to be LSD in my hand."

"That sounds crazy," Jonathon stated in disbelief.

"It's a classic example of a completely inappropriate application of a good idea," Sylvia continued, oblivious to Jonathon's remark. "In high-speed imaging laboratories, psychiatrists and psychologists use the scan to unlock secrets of mental disorders, like, for example, obsessive-compulsiveness."

"Like people with a hand-washing fetish?" Jonathon ventured.

"Yeah, you picked the most common example. Consider those individuals who think obsessively and act compulsively. Consider those who cannot accept anything but perfection in themselves."

That sentence struck Jonathon as if a tumbler of ice water had been thrown on his face. He suddenly realized that Sylvia was describing him exactly. His long walk the previous evening had not produced such an insight. He felt self-conscious but everyone's attention was diverted to the approach to LAX.

"I can't believe how many times I have been back and forth to the Middle East in the past month," Jonathon tried to change his mood with conversation. "I'm not sure my body knows where it is at the moment."

"Let's see, " Sylvia added, as they checked in, "You've gone to Jerusalem for the Bateson trial, then to Atlanta, and then here to Los Angeles."

"To you, " Jonathon found himself saying.

"Exactly. To me, " Sylvia said without hesitation. "My hospitalization, the press inventing a plot making me the Grande Dame of drug trafficking. How ridiculous!"

"You left out Cairo and Mona, before Atlanta," Jonathon was beginning to enjoy himself. Sylvia was disarming.

"And now, here we all are, most of the pieces of the puzzle, all together, traveling back to the Middle East," Sylvia continued. "Don't think about the wear and tear on your body. Think of it instead as a way to have a business meeting between far-flung partners, for that is what we all are."

"Mom, you're psychologizing," Mona chided.

Once on board the jumbo jet and settled in their seats, Jonathon queried, "So you're a psychologist then?"

"Yes, unfortunately," Sylvia responded. "I do have a Ph.D. in the subject, speciality being physiological psychology. I have concentrated my studies since my divorce from Mona's father several years ago, on cures for children's diseases."

The plane took off smoothly and Jonathon and Sylvia shared a drink together. Mona had already fallen asleep.

"One cannot dismiss the biochemical effect of anything," Sylvia continued. "This drink, for example. While it won't alter our personalities, it will disinhibit you to a certain extent, and that could be useful if you were an uptight individual, like those types we were talking about before, the obsessive-compulsives," Sylvia looked pointedly at Jonathon as she spoke.

Ignoring the allusion, Jonathon continued to talk about her work. "Are you familiar at all with the application of LSD as therapy for severe depression?" he asked, searching through his recent acquisition of factoids from the technical papers on the subject which McIntyre had faxed to him for the Bateson case.

"Oh, yes. Actually, that was what began my interest in LSD therapy. It is the structural resemblance of lysergic acid diethylamide, or LSD, to serotonin, which first caught my attention. Serotonin is deeply involved in our sensory perception, of which hallucinogenic activity is a part. In fact, some psychedelics are called 'serotonin psychedelics'-in addition, that is, to LSD-psilocybin, bufotenine, and morning glory seeds."

Jonathon remembered reading those terms in Sylvia's notebook. "As a matter of fact," he ventured, the therapeutic use of LSD was part of my argument in Jerusalem. Bateson was implicated in a conspiracy to sell it, because he had known an individual, a somewhat older man from Wisconsin whom he had met at a rock concert. Bateson had been suffering from untreated depression for many years."

"Let me guess. He started using LSD and it lifted his depression in a more natural way than alcohol, and less destructively, I might add," Sylvia remarked.

"That's right. I had the thought that he was self-medicating."

"Did you state that fact in the defense statements?" Sylvia asked, very alert now.

"Oh yes, very strongly. Here, I'll show you my arguments." Jonathon reached into his briefcase and handed Sylvia a packet of legal documents. "Unless you find that sort of thing boring."

"Don't worry, I'll be selective," Sylvia added, taking the folder without so much as looking at Jonathon. He glanced at Mona, wondering if he should wake her for the lunch that was about to be served. As if reading his mind, Sylvia said, "Don't worry about her. I'll wake her in time. She's always had the appetite of two men."

The lunch was quite generous and Jonathon smiled,

remembering Sylvia's comments, as he handed over his dessert to Mona, who was consuming her food without comment. After the meal, she drifted once more into a deep sleep. Neither Jonathon nor Sylvia seemed interested in the movie.

"Well, I've read your presentation, " she stated as she handed back the court papers. "You got it right."

"Got *what* right?"

"The relationship between LSD and serotonin and dopamine. That's the basis of my theory. With minute daily doses of LSD, the question arises whether the body would then self-correct, by producing more serotonin and less dopamine on its own. In other words, we don't know if LSD would have to be taken therapeutically for many years, or perhaps for the rest of a patient's life, or only for a brief time. Nor do we know the relationship, if any, between LSD and serotonin reuptake inhibitors, like Prozac, for example."

"I find this fascinating," Jonathon remarked.

Sylvia looked at Jonathon, started to say something, then stopped, taking a sip of her wine instead.

"I was only implying . . ." Jonathon began to defend himself just in case she had misunderstood his intentions.

"Yeah, I know," she stated, "but what I prefer to talk about is your obsessiveness."

"My what? Well, I don't know any other way to get a lot of work done, without being obsessive," he replied.

"You realize you're very obsessive? How interesting. When did that happen?"

"My epiphany?" they both laughed. "Actually a short time ago," Jonathon continued. "In Cairo, in fact."

"Why? How?"

"Because. Your son gave me a . . .Oh, I'm sorry. I've forgotten to give it to you. His poem. I've been carrying it around with me. I have it right here."

Sylvia took the now crumbled piece of paper, smoothed it out, then read it silently. Jonathon waited for some comment and not receiving any, was about to take out one of his books, when Sylvia suddenly resumed the conversation.

"You read it, didn't you?" She said.

"Yes. Sorry, I couldn't help it."

"No, that's all right. He wouldn't care. And I certainly don't. He's been writing poems for several years now. He's an extremely intelligent person."

"Does her realize how talented he is?" Jonathon mused.

"Because of *me* he does, yes. His father had a weird belief that people are better off remaining ignorant of their talents. Mona told me yesterday that she was instructed repeatedly by him that she should never tell Tarif how unusually intelligent he really is."

"Strange," Jonathon thought aloud. "His high intelligence would be manifested in his behavior nonetheless, and he would notice the difference between himself and others at some point. Anyone would notice, why wouldn't he? And why shouldn't his own family?"

"Exactly," Sylvia resumed. "It's not that his family should exactly dwell on it, or obsess, if you will, but recognition of a person's identity, including his or her gifts would have been very beneficial. I'm convinced that it would have prevented the reactive depression Tarif developed for several years after he was taken from me."

"By his father, you ex-husband? Who wouldn't agree with your hypothesis, I gather?"

"That's an understatement. He would fly into a rage if anyone seemed to notice how bright Tarif was, even in small things. It was always very awkward when he was around. Like there was some big secret no one was supposed to talk about. We all seemed to be part of a grand conspiracy to deny reality. That's about as unhealthy an atmosphere in which to grow up as I can imagine."

"Full of deception and denial."

"And misplaced protection, too. It's normal for a parent to want to protect his or her child, if it is unusual in any way, but there are limits and drawbacks to too much sheltering. Far healthier in the long run to help a child accept his high intelligence and peculiarities which inevitably accompany it, to make him or her believe that success is possible even though you seem to be different. After all, is there any of us who doesn't have something unusual about us to some degree, either psychologically or physiologically? Which brings me back to your unusual quality, that highly developed obsessiveness."

"That again. Is that why it seems we are destined to be enemies?" Jonathon asked.

"Surely the reason must be obvious. It's almost incestuous. Don't you see?"

"What!"

"What I'm trying to say is that I am outrageously obsessive myself. That's why I can recognize the trait so easily in others. I have fought against it for most of my life, unsuccessfully, I might add."

"I've had very little success myself," Jonathon added.

"But at least I'm aware of it. Obsessives are very difficult people to live with. Doesn't your other half, as they say, try to hint about your obvious imbalance?"

"Other half?" Jonathon laughed. "I'm divorced. There is no other half."

"I know that," Sylvia continued, "Mona already told me. What I meant by your other half was you unconscious."

"I don't pay any attention to irrational thoughts."

"You mean you censor them."

"I have no idea what you mean. Thoughts which are not cohesive nor meaningful are useless and should be dropped. What else can anyone do with them?"

"I'll tell you in a moment. But first, do you dream often?"

"Never."

"Do you drink, I mean, a lot? Because that will inhibit the recall of your dreams, among other things."

"I consider myself to be a moderate drinker. I do remember

some dreams, though. The ones that recur. In fact, two of them returned to me while I was in the Middle East."

"Because your mind-controlling mechanism was a little off balance in a strange environment. Your subconscious had a chance to break through."

"What are you talking about?"

"I'm talking about the other self which is getting annoyed right now because I am focusing on it. Your other self-not the punctual, orderly, proper, self-righteous person you think you are."

"I think I'll have another drink," Jonathon said uncomfortably.

"I'll join you. I'm not trying to denigrate you. I'm simply telling you a story, that's all. It's my story too. Tell me about the dreams you had in the Middle East, the ones that keep coming back, " Sylvia said as she took a long sip of her newly-refreshed beverage.

"If you insist," Jonathon said, warming up to the subject. He was beginning to enjoy the conversation now. He smiled.

"The disinhibiting effects of the alcohol," Sylvia stated.

"Well, far be it for me to take any credit," Jonathon laughed. "I never thought analysis by a psychologist could be so entertaining."

"Analysis, assisted self-examination, whatever you want to call it. It's the best thing for you, better without the alcohol, of course. But we have to start somewhere. Now, the dreams."

"Well. The first one is spooky. I'm lying in the middle of a highway. On my back. I look around and see an ambulance racing toward me on my left. Then I see another vehicle of some sort on my right, also heading toward me. I realize that I am doomed. Either way I try to escape, some part of me will be hit and destroyed."

"And the second dream?"

"The second dream occurred after a long walk while I was in Jerusalem. I usually like to walk to get back inside of myself sometimes, to get my courage back. So, the day before the trial, I walked through the old city, letting off steam, letting the thoughts flow. Later that night I had a dream that I was walking again, in the same vicinity as before. No one was around. As I looked up, I saw a large Grecian vase trembling on the edge of a wall about four stories up on a building I was passing. As it cam crashing down, on me, I was paralyzed. I simply could not move out of its path, until at the last moment, with incredible effort and agony, I pulled myself out of the way. The vase missed me by a few millimeters, crashing into a thousand pieces at my feet."

"You were not harmed, however, in either dream," Sylvia inquired.

"No. You're right. But my recollection is in both dreams that I had narrowly escaped death. You know, I'm really enjoying this, " Jonathon admitted. "It's not every day that I am imprisoned by a psychologist on a 10 hour flight. No fee?"

"None. I happen to believe that dreams are, as Freud thought, the royal road to the unconscious. The way I like to think of them is as expressions of an intelligence deep within us, which never sleeps, like our waking consciousness does. Nor does it forget anything. But it can only speak to us in the language of images and metaphors, while we are asleep."

"Why does it have to speak to us?"

"It works in tandem with our conscious selves. The unconscious integrates what the conscious part gives to it, with the warehouse of memories and motivations which are accessible to it. Your dreams may be telling you, that unless you 'move', read that, that unless you 'change', in some way, you may be in danger."

"What kind of danger?"

"I don't know that. Dreams, as I said, are not specific. They are metaphoric. But psychic danger exists. Maybe it will show up as despondency, perhaps. Or paranoia. A phobia of some sort. It could be any number of things. The message it is giving you in the dream is that your way of construing life, right now, is in need of adjustment."

"Why? It's always worked."

"Nothing stays the same. Change is endemic in life. Your choice is to adapt or perish."

"Sounds pretty black and white to me."

"Yes, it does. But that's how I think of it. I also tend to engage in dichotomous thinking, like you do. Things are either right or wrong, black or white. There is never any gray. It's a very stark world. I have been working hard at this disability of mine for a long time. It is true that the black-and-white way of thinking helps to decipher complex issues clearly and quickly, but it limits the quality of many experiences, of relationships. That's what I meant when I made the comment about you and me. We are so much alike that the possibility of our setting brush fires under our weak spots is a real danger."

"Do you think that might ever change?" Jonathon really didn't care at this point, that his question might be misconstrued.

"Maybe. But change is difficult. Most people grow more like they are instead of changing the way they are. There is a difference. Everyone resists change, don't you think? That's for a good reason. When you change, you lose something of yourself, something in the interim between the old and new selves. That's what I think the meaning of your dream is, when you were lying on the highway."

Jonathon felt an immediate sense of recognition when he heard those words. She continued, "In order to keep abreast of the constant change in life, it's necessary to be a mental trapeze artist, bouncing this trait off that one, and the entire self working toward survival in the unpredictable world it finds itself in. What worked at age thirty might not work at age fifty."

Sylvia turned away. Jonathon realized, that in the past hour, the source of his problem with women. His attitude toward them had not changed since he had been married. He was, in effect, blaming all women for the shortcomings of his former wife. It was a stunning discovery, and it made him wonder what other habits he clung to which were equally outdated.

"It's like excess baggage. Dead space," Jonathon added, then continued, "that's why some people in their seventies and eighties are sharper and younger-appearing, in their thinking, than many of us in our forties and fifties, who 'think' as if we were ninety-five."

He suddenly conjured up the image of Ian McIntyre in his mind. He shuddered to think of it, his rival/hero again. He turned to Sylvia to share these discoveries, only to find that she was fast asleep.

CHAPTER EIGHT

Cairo

All arrivals to Cairo Airport seem the same, thought Jonathon, as Sylvia, Mona and he disembarked in Egypt. Under the unavoidably noticeable pandemonium of the system, somehow people made it to other flights, met family and friends, actually left the airport within two hours of arriving it. That does not appear to be likely when you are at the end of a 100 person line in front of customs. The only thing to do in that situation is to amuse yourself by taking in the scenery. And what a chaotic scene it was. Among out-of-control toddlers and fully armed soldiers you could find lactating mothers, perfectly content to sit along the sidelines chatting for hours with others just like them. Everything looked exactly the same as when he had been there last. His culture shock was gone. However, he still looked as American as Paul Bunyon, and didn't care.

Suddenly from nowhere he heard a familiar voice.

"Ms. Grieg. A pleasure to meet you at long last. Bob Brady, CIA. You are even lovelier than I thought, given the poor quality of agency surveillance photos these days."

Jonathon was surprised to feel a pang of jealousy before he realized that Brady was practicing his McIntyre lessons on how to charm women. "Get to their vanity right away. All else will follow," he recalled one such hint from years ago.

"Why thank you, Lieutenant Brady," Sylvia beamed. "You already know Mona, don't you? As you can imagine, we're all very

tense, considering what is about to happen. Can we go over it
again?"

"Absolutely." responded Brady. "Jonathon and you will be
standing in a special room which we've fitted with a one-way mirror.
We will place Mona at the arrival door for Huzam's flight. It's just
outside of customs, as you know. She often meets him there.
Although Huzam will be expecting his faithful driver, Hassan, he
won't be alarmed to see his own daughter there to meet him."

"That's true," Mona confirmed Brady's facts. "Sometimes I
show up with the driver and sometimes I show up on my own."

"The trick is, " Brady continued, "to keep Hassan off guard.
After all, to his knowledge, you have been away for a few days and
he doesn't know where. That will distract him, since he will be
upset about it, as he considers himself the guardian of the house
and all of its members when the master is gone. Am I right?"

Mona chuckled. "It's true. But you are worrying too much
about Hassan. He considers me an American derelict girl who has
no idea what decent behavior is, someone who kisses taxi drivers as
payment for their rides. He said that to me once! Anyway, I told
him this time that I was going on a camping trip with my friends
to the Sinai, which I often do, and that I wasn't sure whether I
would be back in time to meet Dad at the airport or not. He will
be annoyed to see me here, because it disturbs his perception of
me as being an uncaring fool. In fact, as I left, he gave me a long-
winded speech about how my duty is to meet my father, not to be
out with my friends. It will distract him even more to think that
he has won some brownie points with the "Boss" as he calls my
father. The disgusting sycophant."

Sylvia, Brady, Mona and Jonathon all laughed heartily at Mona's
long-winded exposition.

"Time to get ready," the Lieutenant was suddenly serious and
alert, talking to his nearly invisible phone-piece. "He should be
coming through customs shortly."

Sylvia and Jonathon were taken to a small room outside of the
customs area. An Egyptian guard remained with them, apologizing,

he said, "for your protection, *yanni*." Brady hid himself among the crowd which was gathered there waiting for visitors. Mona placed herself in the front line, so that Huzam and Tarif would see her first.

It had been a long and tiring day for Hassan, the driver and all-around handy man of the Boss. When the family was away, he hired himself out as a driver to the endless tourists who passed through Egypt every day. For his generous wages and tips, he was everything to them: driver, delivery boy, historian, nurse, policeman, interpreter, and sometimes even a baby or pet sitter, which he considered demeaning. It was bad enough to watch a child, which was woman's work, but to have to sit with a dog was absolutely decadent, he though. Most Egyptians regarded dogs as dirty creatures, unfit to live inside the house with the family. Having to go for a walk with one of those pampered American or European canines on a leash was therefore repugnant to him, something he tried to avoid, unless the price was right. For the right price, Hassan would do anything. He was a real Delta felaheen.

That afternoon, he had just completed such a frivolous task for which he was paid a month's wages. He forced himself to walk Mitzi, the Pomeranian, around Cairo. The animal wore a rhinestone-studded collar and leash which he considered a disgrace. How would he ever live this down, he thought. Even the stray alley mongrels seemed to snicker at him, and the street urchins had a field day taunting him. It was with great relief that he signed off his last job and left to pick up the Boss, a man, thankfully, who had his priorities straight, and Tarif, his sometimes wayward son. He would be happy to once again hear the Boss' speeches about solid values and the decadent West, the proper place for men and women . . .and certainly dogs!

He had hoped that Mona would have been home from her camping trip by now. The Boss did not like it when he returned from these trips to find her gone. She was too inconsiderate, Hassan though, too ungrateful of all the correct upbringing the Boss had bestowed upon her, without which, God forbid, what she would have been like. Still the Boss, a good Muslim father, had experienced untold anguish because of this daughter. Why didn't he simply beat her, Hassan though, as he did to his daughters? Righteous discipline builds character and is an honor to receive.

He shuffled along. He hated to be late. It was one thing the Boss could not tolerate in others, although he was often late himself, Hassan noticed. Yet because of the Boss' high position in society, one never questioned. Lateness, when you were part of the upper class in Egypt, was considered a virtue. He had parked the old Fiat in the airport lot and now he was almost running up the stairs to the waiting area outside customs. Then he stopped cold. There was Mona hugging Tarif.

"Ah-hah. Allah Akbar!" he said loudly. "The daughter has mended her ways!" People passing him turned and smiled knowingly. Perhaps her camping trip was sponsored by the conservatives, who would have asked her about her duties to her father. Surely she would not have thought on her own to do the courteous thing.

Suddenly, Hassan was disoriented, uncomprehending what he was witnessing. Six armed guards suddenly came up out of nowhere and surrounded the Boss. Tarif looked confused and terrified. One of the guards took Tarif and Mona by the arm and dragged them off somewhere. The Boss was enraged, but remained oddly calm. Hassan pushed forward in the crowd so that he could reach him. He would rescue his Boss! But when their eyes met, the Boss gave him a slow nod, a sign he always dreaded. It meant, "Do nothing." It had ominous meanings in this situation which he could not fathom. His mind was racing. What was happening?

He nodded back to the Boss, acknowledging, feeling slightly more confident as the Boss managed a slight, calculated smile especially for him, despite being surrounded and being humiliated by the security guards. Hassan thought, "Everything will be all right. He is in charge." There must be some silly mistake. The Egyptians were pushing their weight around. Why? He assumed that the Boss, Mona and Tarif would be questioned together somewhere and the luggage searched. Later they would be released. It's a good thing, he thought, that Mona was there with Tarif, because he would not like being separated from his father.

Then it suddenly occurred to him. The nod! Of course! The Boss had rehearsed it with him so many times. How stupid he was. It was a signal for him to take certain actions which had been gone over many times. Hassan immediately did an about face, raced to the car and drove recklessly back to Maadi, horn sounding all the way, weaving in and out of the traffic. His instructions were in the Boss' safe. He must get to them. People were shouting at him from their cars, swearing at him with their hand gestures, but he did not care. His main job was to save the Boss, to do what the Boss had ordered him to do.

He was instructed about one month ago that if he did everything exactly right, the Boss would be saved forever. He must not change the plan even slightly. He breathed in a full chest of air and thought of Saladin's horse, the stallion. Now it was Hassan's moment in history. People would remember him for years to come, he thought, as he did a 90 degree turn off the highway into the suburb of Maadi, never once considering the stupidity of taking actions the consequences of which he had never fathomed.

CHAPTER NINE

Home

"Well!" the normally complacent Lieutenant Brady remarked, matter-of-factly, "You now have the option of staying overnight here
in Cairo, or turning right around and boarding the next plane for
Los Angeles."

"Los Angeles!" shouted Tarif. He had his arms around his
mother and did not look like he was going to disengage himself
from her for a long time.

"I want to go to Atlanta!" countered Mona. "Mom, I told you
all about Dr. McIntyre's invitation to recuperate, as he called it, at
his home there. And Jonathon is invited too. Please?"

"It doesn't matter to me. I'm curious! But how about Tarif?"
Sylvia ventured in a voice sounding weary.

"I guess I vote for Atlanta," Tarif said, not really caring where
he went, so long as he was with his mother.

"Hooray!" Mona shouted. Cheers echoed throughout Cairo
Airport as Lieutenant Brady congratulated them all and arranged
for them to return to Atlanta.

"But what about Dad?" Tarif paused. "What's going to happen
to him?"

Mona took Tarif aside. They spoke for a while, like brothers
and sisters do, who have shared a difficult period and have survived
it intact. They returned to the group, and Tarif seemed satisfied.
No one really wanted to broach the subject of what was going to
really happen to Huzam. Brady had already told Sylvia and Jonathon
that he would be charged with international trafficking in biological/

chemical warfare. He would be incarcerated for an indefinite time and then eventually brought to trial.

"His probable outcome?" Sylvia asked tentatively.

"Oh, hard to say," Brady answered. "You know how it is in the Middle East. A crime is not always looked upon with the same gravity as it is in other, particularly Western, countries. And he may have connections in high places, at least that's what he kept suggesting to my deputies. The Egyptians seemed unimpressed, though. All my people care about at this point is that we dissolved the chemical drug smuggling ring between Baghdad and Cairo, of which we have had knowledge for a long time. My guess, though, is that he will be let off on some technicality or another, and just lay low for a while. After that, your guess is as good as mine. He is an American as well as an Egyptian citizen. The main thing is that his children are out of his control. We consider him unstable and dangerous."

As they prepared to board, Jonathon remarked, "Returning on another flight back to the United States from Cairo on the same day must be breaking some kind of record. Funny, I'm not at all tired, though. In fact I feel kind of exuberant. What about all of you?"

Sylvia beamed, her arms still around Tarif. "You're finally able to just state how you feel. Progress!". Jonathon beamed, feeling satisfied with himself.

"Tarif and I are just great," Mona spoke for both of them. "I can't wait for Dr. McIntyre to meet Tarif."

Tarif finally spoke out on his own. He blurted out, "What I want to do most, what I've dreamed about, is skateboarding in Trocadero Square, maybe go to a Grateful Dead concert, like I've read about."

Jonathon could not resist his fatherly urges. "You will do those things, Tarif, I promise you."

Once on the plane, Tarif and Mona began experimenting with the head phones, the fax equipment, and the international message system, while Jonathon and Sylvia settled back to relax a few rows behind them.

"You know, Jonathon. You're really making progress. Oh. I've already told you that," Sylvia stated.

"I'm not sure what you mean, but I feel great."

"I mean in allowing yourself not only to feel and experience your emotions, but to be able to express them. To understand that it's okay if your life isn't perfect, if you aren't perfect, in every way."

"The thing is, are you talking about only me, or yourself too?" Jonathon retorted.

"Right. Both of us," Sylvia said immediately. "When I was faced with the desertion of my husband and the loss of my children a few years ago, I did not think I could survive it. Then I discovered it didn't hurt so bad if I worked all the time. I was too tired to think about it. I drove myself, worked long hours, 2 jobs, and finished my research and got my doctorate. But it took its toll."

"How?"

"I was living in a shell. Sure, outwardly, I appeared happy. But inside, a war was going on."

"Between?"

"Between my feelings and my logic. Now do you understand the importance of your dreams? Dreams call attention to the fact that logic is not all there is to life."

"Let me give it a try," answered Jonathon. "The way of life that I had made for myself after my divorce and my brother's incarceration was mechanistic, efficient and productive, but it had no place in it for love or beauty. I do believe that I was always compassionate, though, toward my fellow humans."

"You were telling yourself that, so you could continue living your excuse. Actually you were driven by the need to keep saving your brother, or someone who represented him, over and over again, to prove yourself innocent of his failure to succeed. Weren't most of your clients young men in their early twenties who were convicted of drug offenses?"

"Yes. I agree about that. But you know something, I am not ashamed of that. Because, if my activities were self-serving they also helped those young men to get another start on their lives.

I honestly believe that I made a difference to them and to their families. They were able to see someone in the establishment who could see their side of the story."

"There you go again, back to that preaching, rationalizing mode you are so good at!"

"You are very cruel, " Jonathon said affectionately.

"It's just that," Sylvia offered, "when I chastise you, I am also chastising myself. I told you, in many ways I am exactly like you. The denial. The obsessiveness. The desire for perfection."

"If that's true, how did you solve your problem, if you ever did?"

"Yes, I solved it, thank you. Through a lot of self-reflection and hard work. A good therapist. I disciplined myself to be less disciplined, if that makes sense. I experimented a lot, tried to trick myself out of being my own slave driver. For example, I created a whole wake-up ritual."

"A wake up ritual?"

"Yeah. For you to understand, you have to know how I used to get up in the morning. The alarm clock would have been set for 15 minutes earlier than when I really needed to get up. When it sounded, I literally jumped out of bed into the shower, on the way, hitting the coffee maker to the ON position because I had set it all up the night before with grounds and water and everything, ready to go. Then, while dressing, I would dictate into my tape recorder all of my tasks for that day. After I was finished with that, I would compare what I had dictated just them to what I had dictated the last time I did it, so as not to miss anything."

"Let me guess. That last time you dictated was only the night before as you were trying to go to sleep, but couldn't."

"Right. You are getting the picture. Then of course, I would start coffee-drinking. A cup an hour, not less, sometimes more. Crashing and reviving, all day long. That seemed to be what my days were like. And the worrying. I constantly worried that my children would blame me for what went wrong with the marriage, for what strange behavior they noticed in their father. Of course it was ridiculous. I was the one who was abandoned, not him. But he has a way of insinuating, of suggesting, which places doubts in people's minds about what the truth really is."

"Anyway," she continued," I would say that I accomplished a great deal in terms of personal growth during those difficult years. But I was very lonely. Very unhappy."

"And then?" Jonathon was engrossed in the story.

"Then, I did an about face. Of course, that's easy to do when you are no longer worried about where your next meal is coming from. Whether you can pay next month's rent. You could say the style of a life of desperation needed to be changed to a life of consistency and progress. One of the first things I did was to throw out all of the clocks and scales in my apartment. It's not that time or measurements didn't matter any longer, I just didn't want to be imprisoned by them."

"How did you know the time of day then?"

"I knew. That may sound strange to you. I resumed the long walks of my younger days, when I used to do that to relieve stress and to put things into perspective."

Jonathon was about to interject that he had the same habit, but he asked instead, "Did you have a favorite place to walk?"

"Definitely. Santa Monica beach. That eerie and beautiful juxtaposition of ocean and mountains has always held a deep fascination for me. The mountains symbolize the creative unconscious, of course. The dynamic between them and the sea never failed to imbue me with energy and hope."

"Anything else?" Jonathon ventured.

Sylvia turned to him. "Romance was not needed. This was a solitary journey, remember. Games like romance, can always develop once you have your bearings. It's best not to get involved when you don't know who you are."

"Sounds lonely."

"Of course it does. It is. It's supposed to be. That's part of it. Relationships temporarily blot out the condition of life which is based on boredom and predictability, the main ingredients of our existence. But life comes back to us if we let it. If we can face the fact that ultimately we are alone. That our lives are pointless."

"Harsh. Very harsh," Jonathon responded. "Is there no purpose to a vision in life?"

"The only purpose I've ever been able to realize in life," Sylvia answered, "is the pursuit of beauty and values. You have to believe in them and have the courage to pursue them. Without that, life is meaningless."

"You believe in tradition."

"Hmm. Not necessarily. Tradition means values, true. But not all values are progressive. Some actually hamper individual growth toward self-actualization, toward becoming a fuller human being."

"You're losing me."

"To me, it means allowing expression of all aspects of your self in a healthy way. That should not diminish the expression of someone else's existence."

"This is getting to sound religious."

"Not at all. You're trying to pigeon hole it. In a way it's religious, if you consider the most egregious sin to be the negation of your self. Or the selves of others."

"Where are we now?"

"Somewhere over Dover," Sylvia laughed, enjoying the double-entendre.

"Please continue," Jonathon said, undeterred.

"Okay. Let's say I'm in control of my life now. Finally. Instead of being habituated by others, by mechanical devices which represent those others, like clocks, cars, televisions. I have made a different regime for myself. It's more resonant with my true self than with society. Example: I wake up whenever it happens each morning. I switch on my remote CD player, one of the few machines I allow myself, for the sheer beauty of the music."

"What do you like to hear in the morning?"

"Maybe a Bach. A prelude to Suite No. 1, his unaccompanied cello suites. I play this while I perform mental imagery."

"Funny. I don't know if we mean the same thing by that term,"

Jonathon remarked, "but I use mental imagery to help my prepare courtroom presentations. What's really odd, though, is that I have the same Bach cello suites which I play as I drive along in my car."

"But I don't mean linear imagery, where you rouse yourself to peak performance. I think what I'm striving for if more horizontal, like visual and phenomenological imagery, like free form."

"Mind explaining that?" Jonathon asked, feeling a little drowsy, but still interested,.

"Those Bach suites. Close your eyes and imagine that prelude beginning. Are you into it? Good. Here let me recline your seat for you and put up your foot rest. Are you hearing Bach inside of your head? Keep you eyes closed and imagine entering an underworld park of infinity."

"A what?" Jonathon started to get up from his reclining position.

"Stay down. An underwater park of infinity. Stop interrupting your Bach. Close your eyes. Once you enter this park you notice there are no perceivable boundaries. While you are floating there, you have no fear at all that you might suddenly bump into a boulder, a shark, or a sunken fish, or another person. Yet, when you want to return, all you have to do is to wish it. In fact, one of the prerequisites for admission to the infinity park is to expel all hostility-(think of, 'forgive us our trespasses even as we forgive those who trespass against us')-before you can enter. There are no predators ever allowed inside, not in any form, and certainly not in thoughts, either. No hostile, aggressive thoughts toward another living creature, even one who has hurt you beyond what you can endure. You have no fear of aggression from anyone or anything. Even your breathing is taken care of, for when you pass the entry gate to the underwater park of infinity, you discover that you are able to breath without an oxygen tank."

"Somehow," Sylvia continued, "your body is able to metabolize the oxygen within the water for your needs, like fish do. In this atmosphere of peace and weightlessness, you spiral, you somersault, you float silently or you pirouette among a sea of floating flower petals which change color every few hundred feet, while Bach's crescendos reverberate through your entire being. You have never felt such freedom or peace or beauty before. Your heart sings out with joy, as Bach's cello chords resound louder and louder, approaching the finale. You turn slowly but not reluctantly, to float back through the gate of the underwater park of infinity, just as the last elongated Bach cello note is played."

"You feel incredibly at peace with yourself and with the world. You are not despairing because you had to leave the park of infinity. You know, deep down inside of you, that it is there, anytime you want or need to go there."

Jonathon was fast asleep and Sylvia covered him with two large blankets she found in the overhead bin. Mona and Tarif were watching a movie, yawning. It would be time for dinner soon, but Sylvia was not interested in food. She put her seat back as far as it could go and closed her eyes and heard the distant sounds of a cello.

Atlanta was upon them before they realized they had traveled over an entire ocean. Sylvia and Tarif were wide awake, energized by their curiosity about Ian McIntrye. They landed, gathered their bags and hailed a taxi. Arriving at the McIntyre mansion, there he was, predicably ready, prepared, the perfect host, on the last step, waiting to greet his guests, to hug them, to help them in whatever way he could.

"Mona, at last. I was worried about you. You must be Tarif? And of course, my old student, Jonathon Miracle. This must be Sylvia." McIntyre positively oozed charm and graciousness.

"Please call me Ian. After all, everybody does."

"A little hard," Sylvia admitted, "when you are face to face with one of your idols."

"No idols on this visit. None of that pedantic stuff. Let's just relax and have fun. You must all be exhausted and famished. My faithful housekeeper, Caitlin, has prepared some light snacks and tea. Here, let me take your bags, Sylvia."

Jonathon was looking at his old professor with different eyes. He could see the flirtatiousness of his actions with Sylvia, but he could not get himself to feel bitter about it. What had happened? For an instant, Jonathon recalled a scene from the park of infinity, then it vanished. He realized that he was enjoying himself by simply being himself, and so was Ian. It was a recognition which, far from upsetting him, put him at remarkable ease. He recalled a thought which Sylvia had expressed on the plane: "The greatest existential crime is one of omission, either toward yourself, or toward others."

On a walk in the garden several hours later, McIntyre shared the latest news. "Your exhusband, Sylvia, who has been painted as a villain by the CIA (as you well know), has actually been involved in a many dangerous schemes which we can now discuss, since Mona and Tarif are out of hearing distance."

"What do you mean, schemes?" Sylvia asked, alarmed.

"First of all, he won't be harshly treated. I know you do not wish him ill, that you only want to get your children back. The Iraqi government has disavowed any relationship with him. both it and the Egyptian government are filing charges of attempted murder and premeditated murder against him. Worse, though, is that his houseman, Hassan, was caught at the home in Maadi, preparing syringes of botulin toxin. He had been instructed by Huzam to inject the contents of the syringes-botulism-into the food in the kitchens of certain restaurants. This would not be hard for him to do, given the lax security at these places. The damage this could have caused is catastrophic, as it is the season of Ramadan, when people in Egypt are apt to pay special attention to eating well and eating a lot."

"Good lord, he must be psychotic!" Sylvia exclaimed, horrified.

"Perhaps just dangerously narcissistic. Maybe a little of both," McIntyre continued. "This is a person who believes it is his right to use people until they are of no further use to him, then he destroys them, perhaps not directly, like killing them, but by ignoring them, by refusing to acknowledge them. It is a very good thing for you, Sylvia, that your marriage ended when it did," McIntyre sighed.

Sylvia shuddered and Jonathon mused, "It makes my marital breakup sound like child's play."

"We're not comparing tragedies, " McIntyre chided gently.

"I only meant that truth is always conjectural," Jonathon defended himself.

"Science is never conjectural," McIntyre retorted, very seriously.

"Reality is never rigid. It is always ambiguous!" Sylvia added.

On that note, the threesome of McIntyre, Miracle and Greg joined Mona and Tarif, who were frolicking in the topiary garden, without a care in the world, like the present was all that existed and the future was uncharted, unrestrained, and limitless.

"There is one thing that will never be ambivalent about," McIntyre stated. "And that's lunch. How about a picnic? Caitlin can prepare things while we enjoy our last stroll together."

Mona, Sylvia and Jonathon went off on their own winding path. Ian McIntyre was thrilled to be alone with Tarif at last, who had fallen asleep under a tree. McIntyre motioned the others to go on and closed his eyes for a moment too, leaning against the bark, ever-cognizant of Tarif. At last there was a stirring. "Where is everybody?" Tarif said, rubbing his eyes.

"Off on a walk," McIntyre smiled.

"I must have fallen asleep."

"Well, that's what people do when they have jet lag. You'll be falling asleep at odd times for the next couple of weeks. What a delightful thought!"

"Really?" Tarif asked.

"Yes. Really. Enjoy it."

"Dr. McIntyre, what do you do?" Tarif regarded this ungainly white-haired professor.

"Oh, I read bulletins from other countries every morning. They contain medical statistics and descriptions of diseases which have been recorded by professionals in clinics and hospitals who are paid to do that."

"What for?" Tarif wondered out loud.

"It's to compare one group against another group. Like tuberculosis, for example. You know what that is. Let's say that it's normal for about 1.2% of Americans to get it every year. So we can imagine how many people will be affected the next year. But let's say, we notice that in France, 5% of the people there come down with tuberculosis. We might be able to make a cautious guess about what might happen to Americans the following year, provided certain things happen of course."

"What things?" Tarif wondered, transfixed at this point.

"Because scientists communicate with each other on a regular basis now, I will learn that a certain number of Frenchmen are expected to visit the United States on vacation this year, maybe for a sports event. I have to keep my eye on what is going on in the world of sports, politics, economics, medicine, and in almost every aspect of life and society, between countries. Because all you need is one person with a virus to infect another person. Then it takes off like wildfire, " McIntyre explained.

"We here at the Centers for Disease Control try to anticipate these things before they happen. If we're lucky, we can protect Americans by issuing travel advisories, or suggestions for immunizations, things like that."

"That's really interesting," Tarif remarked.

"Well, I'm glad you think so. It's my bread and butter, so to speak. What do you want to do when you grow up?"

"Oh," Tarif said, self-consciously, "I don't know. I like mathematics a lot. And languages, too. But I don't know if I'd fit in anywhere."

McIntyre probed, "Hmm. Languages and mathematics. That's good. What about music? Do you like music too?"

"I love it, but."

"But what?"

"Well, my father wouldn't let me take music lessons because he said that it wasn't important. I don't think that's true, but.."

"What's not true?"

"I mean," Tarif explained, "my father like music. He would have paid for lessons for me to learn an Arabic instrument, like the Oud, for example, but not an instrument that he regarded as Western."

"Like what?" McIntyre probed.

"Oh, like the cello."

"He didn't like classical instruments?"

"No, he did, but only those associated with Egypt. He didn't like instruments which had their origins in Europe."

"Like the cello, the violin and the guitar?"

"Yeah, I guess so."

"So. You didn't do the Arab instruments, as he wished, " McIntyre mused.

"No."

"Why not? At least it would have been something."

"Because I want to choose for myself. I don't want to study something just because someone thinks I should. I only want to study what interests me."

"That's not a bad way," McIntyre added. "You are probably very good at the things you like to do."

"Like skateboarding, and writing poetry."

"Really!" McIntyre was entranced. "How do you do that?

Tarif laughed heartedly. "Poetry and skateboarding. It sounds weird, doesn't it?"

"Not to me! It seems there's a beat to both activities. Skateboarding may be far more intricate than writing poetry. I wouldn't know because I haven't done either."

"Why don't you try it?" Tarif ventured.

"Why not!" McIntyre shot back immediately. He did not want to lose the opportunity to get closer to the boy. "Unfortunately, I don't have a skateboard here."

"I brought mine with me from Egypt. Do you want to try it?"

"Wild horses couldn't keep me away!" McIntyre exclaimed.

"Let's go!" shouted Tarif. "Wait 'till Mom sees this!"

"I'm going to do this on one condition. That you let me read some of your poems," McIntyre bargained.

"Oh, I don't care about that! Just don't show them to Mona."

"She makes fun of them? It doesn't matter. Get your skateboard!"

Tarif was enervated as he ran back to the house, returning quickly with the psychedelically-decorated skateboard. "You're on your own!" he said as he handed it to McIntyre.

When Mona, Sylvia and Jonathon turned the corner from the glen to the prairie trail, they were astounded by what they saw. There, on the blacktop in front of the McIntyre mansion, was Ian on a skateboard, doing fairly well as he negotiated the driveway and attempted to jump the steps.

"Did you ever think you'd see this?" Jonathon said in shock.

"No. But I think it's great. How old is McIntyre anyway?" Sylvia asked.

"Must be somewhere between 73 and 76, I guess, " Jonathon replied. "But he's always been like this. He's a strange mixture of serious science and adolescence. He's ageless! When I was in medical school, and he was my professor, he drove a motorcycle! And he was in his '60's then."

"You must be kidding," Mona said in awe.

"No, I'm not. He rode his motorcycle every day from his apartment in Cambridge to class."

"He is really cool, Mom," said Mona, without taking her eyes of McIntyre.

"I agree," Sylvia said.

Jonathon was feeling his old rivalry, but he was too happy to be bothered with subjective projections onto Ian McIntyre.

As if she sensed his mood, Sylvia shot Jonathon a glance and said, "Of course, some people have a high valence for transference. Ian is one of them."

"Probably so," Jonathon replied. "I don't really care!"

The week sped by, McIntyre proving to be more discreet at his manipulations of people than Jonathon ever imagined, though his manipulations were benign and usually benefitted everyone. The picnics, the skateboarding, the long walks and discussions, after Caitlin's impeccably prepared dinners came to an end.

McIntyre did not seem disappointed. He said farewell jovially to his guests.

Jonathon whispered to Sylvia on one of their last walks together, "You realize that McIntyre's circle has not been completed."

"No, I don't realize. What do you mean, his circle?"

"I've seen this happen before, " Jonathon confided. "People stay here for a while. McIntyre sort of orchestrates them by creating activities and predicaments which make them think about themselves, their lives, their relationships. Everyone eventually is drawn into it. It's his own private game, if you will. I don't mind it because I think it's harmless. I have no idea what value he places on it."

"He's always in control, you realize?" Sylvia ventured.

The last evening had finally arrived. Caitlin had surpassed herself as chief cook in the McIntyre household. Sitting before the fire, it was difficult to realize that it would all be ending in the morning when Jonathon, Sylvia, Mona and Tarif boarded a plane for Los Angeles. They were all in a way, to begin new lives after their experiences together. The mood was warmly melancholy.

Mona broke the silence. "Dr. McIntyre, I don't know how to thank you for all you have done. I've had a wonderful time here."

"When you visit California, you must stay with us," Sylvia interjected.

"California? Are you all out of your minds? We're going to New York tomorrow. Don't you remember? Mona, you promised me."

"Well," Sylvia interrupted, "New York. I don't know about that. I have to find a school for Tarif and Mona in California. We have to find a place to live. I can't begin to think of all the problems we have yet to face."

Jonathon offered, "You can use my place for a month at least. It's a four bedroom house. I'll be leaving for Indonesia in about a week."

"A stranded youth in trouble?" Sylvia ventured.

"Wrong! I am scheduled to present a paper at the International Association of Criminal Defense Attorneys in Jakarta."

"Hmm,"McIntyre mused, "You can tell us all about that later.

Right now, I suggest that we retire early. You will all find homework assignments in your room."

"What!" everyone shouted in unison.

"That's right. It's nothing you can't handle in a few moments before you fall asleep. And it means so much to me. All of you, including Tarif. You will find an envelope on your desks. Open it up and follow the instructions. It's as simple as that. Then, leave the envelopes with your responses in them in your rooms tomorrow morning, for me. My only request of you is that you do not discuss what was in each of the envelopes for at least a week."

"Okay, fair enough," Jonathon stated.

"You see," McIntyre continued, "I want to read them in peace, by myself, without having all of these precognitions interfering with me."

"I know what you mean," Sylvia smiled.

"I know one thing," McIntyre admitted, "I am becoming more sensitive to the auras of people about whom I care. That may be good or bad, depending on what's happening to them at any particular time. But it is definitely distracting, to say the least. Let's not talk about it any more. Does everyone agree to complete the assignment?"

No one objected, of course. Jonathon walked slowly to his room, opening the door slowly, as if expecting a jack-in-the-box to jump out at him from behind the door. There, on the desk, as McIntyre had predicted, was a white envelope beside a pad of paper and a pencil. He opened the envelope and read.

"Dear Jonathon, It was a pleasure spending time with you once more. I hope you enjoyed it as much as I. You've come a long way since medical school days, when I was your professor. We will, I assure your, see each other again. Tonight, I would like for you to answer the questions on the other side of this page. Use any format you like to answer: prose, poetry, art. Whatever suits you. This is a totally creative endeavor. But when you are finished, please put your response back into the envelope. Reseal it and leave it on the desk. I will collect it tomorrow after you have arrived in California. Thank you, Affectionately, Ian."

Jonathon couldn't turn the paper over fast enough. There, in bold print, he read:

What is it that you want?

The following morning, after his jog, stationary bicycling, and breakfast, Ian McIntyre sat in his favorite brown leather chair in his study, directly beneath the skylight, enjoying a second, particularly aromatic, coffee, which he had ground himself. He awaited Caitlin. At last she appeared, a childish flow emanating from her pleasant, round, face.

"Did you get them all?" McIntyre asked expectantly.

"Oh, yes, indeed. All completed."

"Good. Let's begin then."

"Which one shall we start with?"

"Sylvia."

Caitlin carefully opened Sylvia's sealed envelope. It was a ritual she had performed for several years as part of her responsibilities of employment for Dr. Ian McIntyre, Nobel Laureate, famed neurophysiologist. She squared her shoulders and read:

"I want, hopefully on New Year's Eve, to dance with a man who is my ideal and equal in every way."

"That's it?" McIntyre said in obvious surprise.

"I'm afraid so. No further comments, nothing."

"Hmm. A pity. It seems serendipitous. I had expected more. What do you make of it?"

"Well, " Caitlin began, "It's hard to say, but I think Sylvia has come full circle, in a way."

"I think I see what you mean. Yes. I see it now. She began her adult life in a way which was too finished. She had the husband, children, the dog, the station wagon. When she lost all of that she was confronted with her real self and realized what she had to do. She is what is commonly called 'a late bloomer. The romantic ideal in her became jaded, tarnished, by her husband. Faced with the rigors of survival in a reality too harsh for what she was prepared, she was forced to relinquish her naivete. Of course, she does not completely lose her sense of idealism. She banishes it only temporarily, while she shores up her other strengths which have been lying dormant for so many years, neglected, one of which was her intellect, which needed discipline."

"I quite agree, " Caitlin chimed in, "But she did a good job of it, don't you think? A Ph.D. in three years? Mastering physiologic psychology . . .starting from scratch at age 40? Is that not laudable?"

"Quite. So the intellect takes over. Emotions are shunted to the back burner, but never extinguished. Then the denouement."

"And?" Caitlin asked.

"And, she returns once more to the idealism which spawned her into the world. Haw resilient is the human spirit. She returns to her romanticism."

"It doesn't matter where, it only matters that she moved," Caitlin added.

"She's an ingenue. Yes. Her further development in the next year should be interesting, don't you think, Caitlin?"

"With her children and idealism recovered? Nothing can stop her!"

"And your prognosis?" McIntyre ventured.

"The formation of the whole self, very soon."

"I agree, " McIntyre stated. "Who's next?"

"Hmm. Miracle," Caitlin stated hesitatingly. " Handwriting erratic, sloping downward. He uses so many word to describe or perhaps to disguise what is so simple. He wants to defend the most complicated criminal cases so as to.."

"To win, of course."

"I disagree," Caitlin pronounced. "There's been a change in Jonathon. He states, so as to shed the burden of his brother's destiny."

"Remarkable! Progress at last. Illumination. Of course it was Sylvia who did that to him. He wants to change but doesn't know how. He's standing on a precipice. The dissolution of his marriage occurred simultaneously with an awakening of his true self.

The new self was stuck with all this old baggage, guilt, blame, regret. Still, I have great hopes for Jonathon. How about you?"

"Of course, he was always one of my favorites," Caitlin concluded.

"Yes," McIntyre continued, "but he must shed that hard, concrete-like encasement of virtue and sense of proper conduct and rely on his soul to guide him! His soul is good, not evil. He must learn to trust it. He has been bullied most of his life by his harsh conscience, like a jailer. People will use him, sensing his altruism."

"Prognosis?" Caitlin asked.

"Hard to say," McIntyre responded. "He is very taken with Sylvia: her intelligence and courage to surmount despair and anguish, to rely on discipline and organization as tools to stabilize her life. He has not been tested to the degree that she has, but he wants to be. Everything for Jonathon is in the context of his brother's incarceration. He must free himself of that."

"Can't you be more optimistic?" Caitlin asked.

"No."

"Okay. Next. Mona. She wrote, "I want an intact family. I want my mother and father to get along. They are both remarkable people in their own ways. I don't want hate to be part of my life. I want my brother Tarif to be able to live out his life as he chooses. His intelligence shines forth. I want my mother to find peace, soon. I wish for my father to go beyond greed and ego-satisfaction, which destroyed his marriage to my mother. I want him to find true happiness.""

"She's not talking about herself at all," McIntyre remarked. "But fortunately, her security resides in an orderly progression. When the ones she cares for in her life are settled, then she will be able to move forward. She cares too much. It is a blessing and a curse. If she can hold out until her mother, Tarif, and the father get their acts together, she will positively soar. She is a diamond in the rough."

"And now, Tarif," Caitlin announced. "I don't know what to make of this. It's a running monologue."

"Just read it as it is, " McIntyre stated.

"I am a prisoner of my own vortex. I have created the tomb in which I dwell. My parents have no idea what life is all about, certainly not mine. They are consumed with ideas of self-aggrandizement and profit. They miss the true meaning of just about everything. It's always staring them in the face. Become. Become. That is life. I feel it strongly. I feel like behaving in ways that people around me would think strange. I have to choose. I am always stopping myself. I have made up a person, who is not really me, who deals with others who observe me. This person is tough. He can beat others as well as joke afterwards. What I want, most of all, is to experience a relationship where someone knows me as I really am. I am my thoughts. I am my time. I am my choices."

There was a long silence before either McIntyre or Caitlin could speak. Finally McIntyre ventured, "Tarif, you are the most crystalized of all the four who came before you. The pain you have suffered, the social discrimination, the ostracism, have welded your soul into a glistening sheath of formidable strength. You are still at risk. There is no way to warn you. The risk is the attraction of a pseudo-acceptance by a person or by a group which is beneath you intellectually, but which offers you acceptance and recognition. In a way, there is a parallel with Jonathon Miracle here. Acceptance is needed, eventually, at any cost, save annihilation."

"Tarif needs a guru, a wise guide who will give him both freedom and respect, two different qualities which must reside within the same mental domain. Yet, of all the four, he holds out the most promise."

"Why?" Caitlin asked.

"Because he has been shaken to the core. The others maintain a semblance of self-respect if not egotistical self-delusion. Tarif has looked at the impermanence of existence, straight in the face, he recognizes the illusionary quality of love, and its most horrible consequence, exploitation of another."

Caitlin quietly gathered the sheets of papers on which were written the intimate thoughts of each of their guests.

"And shall I put these in the 'personality safe' along with all the others, Dr. McIntyre?"

"Yes. These we will keep. We have to follow up on them. Isn't that what a good scientist does?"

THE END

LaVergne, TN USA
13 December 2010
208581LV00007B/162/A